VANESSA
NORTH

roller
girl

A Lake Lovelace Novel

RIPTIDE
PUBLISHING

*To Courtney*

*"Every body is good at derby, and has a place."*
—Jude E Boom, Boulder County Bombers

# TABLE OF contents

# chapter ONE

**d**oesn't every girl dream of waking up to a face full of water and Elvis standing over her, his rhinestones a-glittering and his tongue all hanging out?

When the shock of it wears off, I turn on the light.

Oh God, I'm not dreaming. My dog is soaking wet and standing on my bed.

I rub a hand across my face and blink up at him.

"Did you tip over your bowl, baby?"

He shakes out his coat again, and it hits me that he's *really* soaked. Not paw-in-the-bowl wet, but fell-in-the-lake wet. At one in the morning.

"Down, Elvis," I order, sitting up.

With a whine, he jumps to the floor and starts rolling on the carpet to dry himself. My bed is drenched. Jesus. I'm going to have to wash the sheets. At one in the *morning*.

"Thanks, Elvis." I glare at him.

He wags his tail. Damn, it's hard to stay mad.

"Come on." I pull on my robe, and Elvis follows me through the house but stops before we get to the kitchen and starts whining.

Of course I don't take the hint. One step onto the tile floor and I'm flat on my ass—with a splash.

Water, everywhere.

The kitchen is flooded; water's pouring out from—the washing machine? Oh God, I'm useless at fixing things. People? Bodies? I can work with. But *things*?

Nope.

Lisa would have known what to do. Lisa could fix anything. It hits me like a fist in the stomach—Lisa isn't my wife anymore, and she isn't ever going to fix anything for me again. Sitting on my ass in cold, soapy water, I actually think about calling her. Yeah, that conversation would be fun. I can hear it now.

*Oh, hi, Lis! I know it's the middle of the night and you hate my guts for killing your husband, but can you tell me how to fix the stupid front-loading washing machine I bought you for our anniversary?*

Nope.

No calling Lisa.

I'm so fucked.

I run through the list of people who are still talking to me who might know what to do and who would answer their phones in the middle of the night. Eddie—but he'd just wave his wallet at the problem, and I don't need money; I need someone to tell me what to do. My dad? No, not unless I want him to talk to me like I'm three instead of thirty-eight.

*Ben.*

One in the morning. I cringe, but I dial anyway.

"Tina?" His voice is sleep-slurred. I'm an asshole. "You okay, sweetheart?"

"My washing machine flooded my kitchen. What do I do?"

There's a long pause.

"Ah, shit. Um. Turn off the electricity at the breaker—in the garage. You know what it looks like?"

"Hold on." I go out to the garage and glance around. Elvis, unwilling to follow me across the wet floor—not that I blame him—whines. "No. What does it look like?"

"Gray metal box, flush to the wall."

I spy it peeking out from behind boxes of Lisa's stuff. "Yeah, found it." Moving a box out of the way, I open the panel to see the rows of switches. "Okay, now what?"

"Anything to do with water should be labeled. Actually, if the electrician who wired your house was a super-nice guy, they should all be labeled." They are. Thank goodness for super-nice electricians. I find the one that says "Laundry" and flip the switch.

"Okay, electricity off. What now?"

"Unplug the machine. Get the clothes out and into buckets—like five-gallon paint buckets. If you don't have buckets, maybe put them in the bathtub. Dry the kitchen up as best you can and call a repair person."

Okay, I can do that. I can handle that. "You're a lifesaver."

His distinctive, bold laugh fills my ear. "Nah, that's you. Wouldn't be here if you hadn't come to borrow my electric screwdriver that night. Telling you where to find your breaker is the least I can do."

I swallow around a lump in my throat at the memory, and then it hits me. Ben's party is tomorrow—yeah, maybe it's weird to celebrate his sobriety with a party, but it's damn well worth celebrating. "Your thing is tomorrow?"

"I understand if you can't come." His voice is soothing, easygoing. He really does understand, and he doesn't hold grudges.

Like I'm not going to be there though? No way I'd miss even a normal day on the lake with my best friends, let alone one that means so much to all of us.

"I'll call you in the morning and let you know what the plan is with the repair person, but hell or high water, I'm planning to be there."

He laughs again. "I think you got the high water covered. Okay, T. Call me later. G'night."

I hang up the phone and go to face the mess.

Lisa used to make all the phone calls. Doctor appointments—except the ones I didn't tell her about—restaurant reservations, vacation plans, all of it. She took care of everything because I didn't like to, didn't want to, hated talking on the phone. I've never had to handle something like this before—not once in my life. I went from my mother's house to my wife's and took their organizational skills for granted.

Dread settles into my stomach just past dawn as I reach for my phone, my hand shaking. A quick Google search pulls up dozens of plumbers. How do I know which one to choose? How did Lisa always know these things? How shitty an adult am I if I can't even handle the basics of living alone? Lisa had called a plumber once for a leak in the bathroom—maybe she'd kept a receipt?

At first glance, the desk in the kitchen looks almost the way she left it. There's still a pile of mail on it, now months old, and a coffee cup, the broken handle long gone, holding mismatched pens and pencils. Even a spare pair of her sunglasses sits near the edge. She always went for the oversize aviators—I like sporty mirrored lenses better. I could call her, let her know they're here—maybe arrange for her to come pick them up. Or we could meet for coffee and I could hand them over. There's a little flutter in my chest at the thought of seeing her again, before it spikes into pain.

No. She wouldn't appreciate me calling her and dredging up all our fucking *feelings* only to hand over a pair of sunglasses she bought at Target for $14.99. I put them on my head instead, to hold back my hair, and I open the drawer.

There, taped to the bottom, is a list.

Her mom's number. My mom's number, crossed out and replaced with my dad's. Elvis's veterinarian. My gym. Her old office. And then, the gold mine:

Utilities. Landscaper, gutter cleaning company, cable, gas, electricity, and below it electrician. Then Lake Lovelace Water and Sewer Authority, and below *that,* plumber, crossed out with a note *pricing not competitive,* and below it, two more numbers and, in Lisa's careful, rounded handwriting *24-hour emergency line* with a circle around one of the numbers.

Marrying Lisa was one of the smarter things I've ever done in my life, which is kind of ironic because it was also one of the stupidest things I've ever done in my life.

I dial the number.

Twenty minutes later, I've got an appointment "between eight and ten" for a guy named Joe to come fix whatever caused the washing machine to flood.

I hang up the phone and the panic sets in. A stranger in my house. In my personal space. God, I hate living alone.

A trick of the light and someone decides my jaw is too square or my voice too deep—am I strong enough to defend myself if something goes wrong? Is Elvis a deterrent? He's not exactly a *big* dog. Ben—I could call Ben. Again. No, shit, I can't call Ben. He's got his party today. That's okay. I can do this myself. I'm a big girl.

The first time I was catcalled and followed down the street, Lisa found me crying in the shower afterward. She told me all women fear male violence, but that if we really stopped to think about it, we'd never get through the day. I didn't learn that lesson as a teenager; I'm still at the stopping-to-think-about-it stage.

So even though it's god-awful early in the morning and I've been hauling buckets of water-logged clothes around my house half the night, I pull out my makeup box and get to work.

Putting on makeup is comforting routine to me now, like putting on armor before going out in public. Contouring, highlighting, concealing. Eye shadow—but not too much. Blush—because all that contouring and highlighting leaves me with the complexion of a mannequin. As a little girl, I played with Mom's makeup, but unlike the other girls, I didn't get a trip to the Clinique counter when I was thirteen to learn how to do it right. I got yelled at by my dad and disgusted looks from my brother.

When I finally braved the MAC counter in my late twenties, a sweet fem boy with skin like porcelain and empathy for days taught me all his tricks—and YouTube taught me everything else.

Except lipstick. I still use the same cherry-flavored lip balm Lisa wore when we were kids, and every time I put it on, I remember falling in love.

Tina fucking Durham, badass extreme athlete, hard-ass personal trainer—and cherry-flavored lip balm addict. Ready for anything, up to and including forced social interaction with a stranger.

Hopefully, the plumber will figure out in a hurry what caused the flood, and I can be out on the boat with the guys by noon. I send a quick text to Ben—who I am *sure* is awake by now—fix the coffee, feed Elvis, and take him for our morning walk.

Elvis tugs at the end of his pink sparkly leash and whines. Usually, we'd run a mile or so at the beginning of the walk to get my heart rate up and maximize the efficiency of the workout, but *usually* I wouldn't be armored up with my best contouring, just in case the plumber is a big ol' 'phobe.

When we get back to the house, Elvis's tongue is lolling out and the plumber's van is parked outside. Early. Wow. That's . . . unexpected.

"Sit," I order as the van door opens, and Elvis drops his back end to the ground.

A woman hops out of the van, and I do a double take. Petite, with short black hair that flops in her eyes, and a pierced nose. Baggy, cutoff camouflage cargoes hang low on her hips, and a white ribbed undershirt shows off swirls of colorful tattoos on her arms. Holy shit, she's *cute*. She flashes me a quick smile and starts talking, fast.

"Hey, I'm Joe Delario. Joanne, actually, but everyone calls me Joe. I'm sorry I'm early, but since it's Saturday and you're the only appointment I've got today, I figured we could knock it out, get it done, get on with our lives, right?" Her voice is raspy, like that of a lifelong smoker. Her cheeks dimple as she grins at me and extends her hand.

"Tina Durham." I clasp it in my own. It's delicate but callused, and bright blue polish is chipping off her nails. "I've um, never met a female plumber before." I immediately blush, because God, I should know better than to say shit like that.

She laughs, a hoarse chuckle that lilts up in pitch at the end. "Yeah, it's such a sausage fest in this industry, but the money's good. Can't let the boys get it all. Plus, my dad is a plumber, and he never wanted me to have to depend on a dude for anything, so he taught me and I kind of inherited the business. Not that he's dead. Just retired." She lets go of my hand and holds hers out to Elvis. He sniffs, glancing at me out of the sides of his eyes.

"Hey, buddy, what's your name?" When he doesn't show any signs of aggression, she drops to a squat and starts scratching his ears. "Okay if I give him a treat? I like to make friends with the pooches on my jobs. Makes life easier."

"Sure. He's Elvis."

"Hiya, Elvis." She reaches into one of the cargo pockets on her cutoffs and fishes out half of a dog biscuit. "You're a good boy, aren't you? Yeah. You like that? Who's a good dog?"

My heart lurches as I watch her make kiss faces at Elvis, fishing out the other half of the biscuit and handing it over. After he crunches it to pieces, he butts her hand with his head, begging for more scratches, which she delivers with good-natured efficiency. I'm getting a little emo—it's not only that she's nice to dogs, it's that she plans ahead to be nice to dogs.

Humming "Suspicious Minds" under her breath, she stands and opens the back of her van and starts pulling out tools. She buckles a belt around her waist, then grabs a bucket full of other tools and calls over her shoulder "So, are you a big Elvis fan? I mean, you named your dog after him. Presley, not Costello, right? I mean, it could be Costello, but you strike me as a Presley kinda girl."

I have no idea what a "Presley kinda girl" is, but she nailed it. And she was just humming one of my favorites. "Yeah, Presley. How could you tell?"

"The rhinestone leash and collar. Okay, let's do this thing." She slams the back of the van shut, and Elvis jumps. "You told our dispatcher it was the washing machine? You have kids?"

I follow her up the steps of my house, then unlock the door for her. "No. I'm not married. I was, but my—" I take a deep breath, then muscle through the coming out like it's no big fucking deal. "—my ex-wife and I didn't have any kids."

"Gotcha, okay." She nods briskly. "Baby clothes can be a culprit in these cases. Well, I guess I gotta work for it this time." She flashes another megawatt smile. "Where am I headed?"

I point to the laundry closet off the kitchen. "It's in there. Can I get you a cup of coffee? I can start a new pot?"

"Nah, I had an energy drink in the van. You go on and do whatever you normally do on a Saturday morning. I got things covered over here."

It strikes me when she says "energy drink" that she reminds me of Ben, with all her enthusiasm and easy humor. I can totally see her trash-talking while watching a game with him, or arm-wrestling over the kitchen counter. I shake away the mental image just as it makes me grin.

"Okay, I'm gonna work out then. I'll be down there." I gesture toward the hall. "Last door on the left. If you need the restroom, it's the first door on the right."

"Sweet, thanks. I'll come find you when I have you all fixed up."

"Hey." Her voice comes from behind me, that gritty rasp sending another spark through me. Setting down the dumbbell, I glance over my shoulder.

She's leaning against the doorframe, pink from exertion, hips cocked forward and arms crossed over her chest. She smiles when I catch her eye, and she holds up something tiny, wet, and covered in black shit.

"Found the culprit. Running socks, man. They're as bad as baby socks for getting in your drain and clogging it up. This one's been in there a while—it was really only a matter of time."

Relief washes over me. A stuck sock. I don't need a new washing machine.

"That's it?"

She shrugs. "You might want to get a lingerie bag to wash little stuff like this in, but yeah, your machine is fine."

"Thank God." I wipe a bead of sweat from my forehead and stand up. "Do you take a credit card? Or should I write you a check?"

"I've got an app that takes cards." Her eyes focus over my shoulder. "Holy shit, are all those yours?"

I glance back to see what she's looking at. Ugh. *My trophy wall.* Row upon row of mostly second-place trophies with my dead name on them.

"Yeah. I used to be a pro wakeboarder." My face gets hot—not from embarrassment, but something else, something I have a hard time pinning down. "A long time ago."

"That is so fucking cool." She peeks around my home gym. "Why'd you stop? You're not that old. I'm sorry, I'm being totally nosy. And unprofessional. Sorry for the f-bomb, but it's not every day you meet a pro athlete."

"*Former.* I had some growing up to do." I tamp down on the sudden urge to tell her how wakeboarding was my own personal fairy godmother, but how the Disney-fied versions of the old stories get it wrong: getting your wish come true doesn't happen just because you're virtuous and sing to animals. Wish fulfillment comes at a price. The tournament that paid for huge parts of my transition was the last one I ever competed in.

No regrets, not *exactly*. Not like Ben, who misses it so bad you can see it on his face every time he looks at the lake. Sometimes, though, I miss the thrill of competition and the camaraderies and rivalries that sprang up between friends. The sport was a huge part of my life and now it isn't, and won't be. Sure, I've toyed with the idea of going back, but my days as a pro are long over.

"Oh." She looks down at her feet, quiet like she's picked up on my weird vibe. "Sorry."

I shrug. "Let's get you paid."

Back in the kitchen, she takes my card and swipes it, then hands me a stylus to sign her phone.

"Okay, so now that you're not my customer anymore, want to come grab some breakfast with me?" She bites her lip on a flirtatious half smile. The force of it hits me like I caught an edge on a double up. Heat runs up my spine. Yeah, I want breakfast with her. And maybe a coffee-flavored kiss and to run my hands through that floppy hair to feel if it's soft.

Having sexual thoughts about someone other than my ex-wife is such a novelty that I stand there and stare at her for a moment like a deer in the headlights.

Her smile fades. "Nah, never mind. I just thought . . ."

"I would love to." I wince. "But I can't. I have . . . a thing. A prior commitment. My friend Ben—it doesn't matter. I can't today. But I want it. Want you. *Shit.* Want to see you."

Elvis comes and stands between us when I curse, full on protective mode engaged.

Joe laughs, reaching into her pocket for another dog biscuit, which she hands over, and he collapses to the floor, snorting delightedly as he devours it.

"How about a drink then? You free tonight?"

"Tomorrow would be better. I didn't sleep much last night." I gesture to the washing machine. "I'm going to turn into a pumpkin by eight."

"All right. Tomorrow, Tina." She bites her lip again, and I feel that lurch-tug of attraction. "I'll put my number in your phone."

Somehow, we manage that exchange with the bare minimum of awkwardness, and then I'm watching her drive away.

Holy shit, I have a date.

I'm *dating*.

# chapter TWO

**b**en and Dave's house is so pretty, all glass and stone and wood—it's totally the outdoorsy dude version of Barbie's Dream House. Dave's an architect, and talented. Glancing around, I take in the massive fireplace and the furniture that probably cost more than my car—no matter how many times I visit, the room still takes my breath away. It looks like something out of a magazine, and I always feel weird having a key to a place this glamorous. My parents had a lake house when I was a little girl, but ours was more rustic weekend cabin than dream house. I hold tight to Elvis's leash as I let myself in the front door, then lock it behind me. His toenails click cheerfully against the hardwoods as we cross the gorgeous living room to the glass door leading out to the backyard—this one is unlocked, and I leave it that way after passing through.

Elvis whimpers as we skirt the swimming pool and head down to the dock, though he doesn't full-on balk until we get out over the water. Then he barks his betrayal at me in full voice. Poor pupstar. I wish I had some of Joe's dog biscuits in my pocket to soothe him.

Dave's Nautique idles at the end of the cove, and another boat is cruising along the side where Dave's little brother—Ridley Romeo, reigning wakeboarding champion—and his friends built a rail. The top of Ridley's blond head is just visible in the passenger seat.

"Sit," I order—firmly, because Elvis hates water and might bolt at any moment—and wave at Dave's boat.

When they pull up to the dock, I pick Elvis up by the handles on his life jacket, and as I hand him across to Ben—who hauls him into the boat and sets him on the floor to scurry under Eddie's feet—I greet my buddy with a "Hey, baby" and a kiss on the cheek.

"Hey, T." Always a gentleman, Ben's boyfriend reaches out to help me into the boat.

"Hi, I'm Wish. I'm with Eddie." A tall, muscular stranger waves at me from the sundeck.

I have to do a double take as I shake his hand. He can't be more than twenty-five—not who I would have expected for Eddie's date. His type generally seems to lean more toward burly, leather-wearing bears.

Eddie is sprawled behind the wheel. Dark red-and-purple bruises curl up from the back side of his thighs in angry stripes. I raise an eyebrow, and he gives me a smug little smile.

"We were chatting about the differences between snowboarding and riding wake." Ben draws my attention back to Wish. "He's a snowboarder."

I sit down on the sundeck and look at Eddie's date again, all scruffy and cute, eager as a puppy dog, and I try not to picture him putting those marks on Eddie.

"Ben was just telling me about how sliding on your edges helps you learn to jump. I figured out how to slide heelside, but maybe you can show me toeside?"

"Sure." I start getting into my gear. "Hey, Eddie, I'm gonna demonstrate the backside slide for Wish. Give me a pull?"

I turn back to his date, "You know how you dig your toeside edge into the snow when you're facing uphill on a snowboard?"

"Yeah, sure."

"Same deal when you're facing away from the boat—dig that edge in to set the board into a slide. Don't let your heelside edge catch or you'll smack the back of your head on the water so hard your ears will ring." I turn to Ben "Lube?" Of course, they all snicker as he hands it to me.

Once my feet are slicked with lube and shoved into the bindings, I grab the handle and jump into the water, gesturing for Eddie to pick up the slack.

In a moment, the rope starts dragging me forward, and I scrunch my body and ease to a standing position. I feel out the water—a little choppy from all the activity in the cove—and turn my board until my back is to the boat, digging my toeside edge into the water and sending a spray up behind me. I turn around, demonstrate moving into the slide a few more times, then face forward again as Eddie signals he's going to turn the boat.

I love this part—flying. I swing wide to the outside as he prepares to cross his own wake. The double-up is huge, and I aim straight for it.

I've never been afraid of the big wakes. Not when I was a kid, not when Ben got injured—never. There is nothing in the world like the thrill of being launched into the air. I've *missed* this since I gave up riding professionally.

When I hit the wake, I throw my hips back and spin with the rope held over my head. I keep it simple, a single full rotation, then pull the handle down to my hips and bend my knees into the landing.

The guys on the boat erupt in cheers, and I can see Ben start to explain what I've done, all big gestures and grins. I wave to Dave and drop the rope. As I sink into the water, Dave motions to Eddie to turn, and they come back to pick me up. In the boat, Wish is already pulling on the vest and shoving his feet into the bindings of Ben's board.

I envy him—it's been a long time since I tried something new—but his excitement is contagious, and I can't stay jealous. Instead, I bask in the sunshine with the company of my best friends in the world, and wonder what Joe is up to.

Later, we move the party into the backyard. I pull a chair up next to the grill, watching Ben cook while Eddie and his date dance in a corner of the yard. Elvis collapses at my feet, side-eyeing the swimming pool.

"Hey, buddy." Ben glances over. "How's the washing machine?"

"Fixed." I take a sip from my soda. "By the cutest little butch ever."

"Awwww, hell." He grins at me. "Tell me more."

I shrug. "She gave me her number, invited me out for a drink. We'll see."

"Good for you." He studies the meat on the grill for a minute, then looks at me again. "You do okay with the anxiety? I thought about offering to come over when you texted, but you didn't ask, and . . . Well. I didn't want *you* to think *I* didn't think you could handle it."

"It was good. *I* was good. And of course, not to be sexist or anything, but once I saw Joe was a woman—it's Joanne, by the way—I felt totally safe."

"I don't blame you there. Glad she fixed up your machine. What happened to it?"

"Running sock got caught in the drain and clogged it up."

"Son of a—" He shakes his head. "I should check ours and make sure nothing's stuck in there."

"Yeah, you should."

"So you're going on a date." He glances over at Eddie and Wish, who are grinding together and whispering in each other's ears like they're alone in the world. "Seems to be a bunch of that going around."

"I like him." I gesture at Wish with my chin. "He can hold his own with Eddie, not let him get his way all the time."

"He's a kid." Ben grunts.

"Like Dave isn't ten years younger than you? Oh wait—are you jealous?" I tease. I've known Ben and Eddie for a long time, but this is a side of their friendship I haven't seen before—Ben getting all territorial?

"Naw. It ain't like that. I just don't want to see him get hurt. You neither."

"I'm only going out for a drink with a pretty girl."

"You always did like the pretty girls." He swats a mosquito away from his face. "Have fun, okay? But be careful."

I stand up and wrap my arms around him in an awkward sideways hug. "Of course, baby."

He lets me hug on him for a minute—Ben's one of those guys who seems to have a hard time believing he deserves affection—before he squirms away with a blush and a smile.

"I mean it though. You haven't dated anyone since Lisa. And I don't want to get all lecture-y or anything, but more's changed than your plumbing, you know? Dating isn't like it was when we were kids."

My cheeks flush. "Ben, if you give me a dental dam speech, I sweartagod I won't speak to you for a month."

"Dental-what? Oh, hell, that's not what I— Oh man. No. No. No. No." He digs the heels of his hands into his eyes and groans. "I mean yes, by all means, use whatever protection—can we go back to what I was saying?"

"For the love of everything holy, please do."

"I just meant that you don't know this girl, her friends, family, anything about her. People are weird about gender stuff—if you're ever scared for your safety, call me, okay? And if you don't get me, call Dave. No questions asked, we're here for you."

A lump forms in my throat and I hug him again. "Thank you." This time, he puts his arms around me and squeezes me back.

# chapter THREE

t he bar Joe chooses, Blue's, is one of those run-down dives in a strip mall, dark and sort of sleazy. My heart sinks a little. I'm not a snob about these things, but it's not exactly the kind of place you choose if you're trying to impress a date. Inside it's full of neon and country music. The scent of years of indoor smoking still clings to the wood and carpets. A handful of men play darts by the back wall, and a cute bartender with a red afro smiles to herself as she types into her phone. She glances up when I walk through the door, lifts her chin at me, and waves to a booth in the back.

And there she is.

Joe's ditched the men's undershirt and cutoff camo cargoes and replaced them with skinny jeans and a button-down. Small hoop earrings glint in her ears, and if I'm not mistaken, she's put on a little makeup. The softer style is sexy on her, and it does something warm and twisty to my insides to realize she dressed up for me. She stands as I approach and gestures for me to sit at the booth.

"Wow." I grin at her as I slide into the seat. "You look really nice. I mean, you looked cute in your beater and cutoffs too, but this—you're so pretty."

She closes her eyes when she smiles, an unconscious, girlish gesture. How old is she? I'd guess early thirties, but I've never been good at guessing women's ages.

"Thanks for coming." She sits across from me and takes a sip of her beer. "I don't usually ask girls out who I meet on the job, so this is a little weird for me."

"You gotta admit, hooking up with the plumber is definitely a porno meet-cute."

She snorts and spills her beer. "Wow, um. Yeah. You just said that, didn't you?"

"I can't help it; most of my friends are dudes. I've gotten used to talking like we're in a locker room all the time."

The bartender appears at my shoulder, dropping a coaster on the table in front of me. "So, Joe's friend. What'll you have?"

I glance up at her, and her smile isn't a fake "I work in the service industry" smile, but a genuine smile like she's happy to see me. It's contagious; I grin back.

"Something hoppy, draft if you got it, please."

"We've got a local IPA—brewed right down the road."

Lake Lovelace Brewing Company is the only brewpub locally—Eddie's family used to be part owners, but he sold out about ten years ago. "That would be perfect, thanks."

"You got it." She sashays away.

"You like hoppy beer and say please and thank you to the wait staff. Marry me."

I glance at Joe. "So, you're friendly enough with the bartender that she knows your first name. You come here a lot? I have to admit it's not exactly what I expected."

She covers her blush with her hand and shakes her head. "Oh God, it wouldn't be, would it? This place is . . . Stella's a good friend. If I'm going out, I might as well come here, you know? Plus, the fried pickles are amazing."

Stella reappears with two beers in hand, sets one in front of Joe and the other in front of me. "Yeah, the fried pickles." She smiles at Joe. "Anything else from the bar menu?"

"Get the pimiento cheese fries—they're my second favorite," Joe stage-whispers.

"I guess I'll have those," I tell Stella.

"Good choice."

I raise my glass to Joe. "Cheers."

"Cheers." She clinks her glass against mine and we each take a deep drink. My beer is bitter and cold and absolutely perfect.

"Fried pickles and pimiento cheese fries. I'm going to have to do an extra couple miles on the treadmill after work tomorrow."

"What do you do?" Joe asks, her blue eyes dancing over the rim of her beer. "Now that you're not a pro wakeboarder."

"I'm a personal trainer. I mostly work with people getting in shape after years of not being active, help them set appropriate goals so they don't get injured. I've got a few bodybuilding clients too, which is fun in a different way—hence the extra treadmill time. I have to look the part to sell my services."

"I bet that's a rewarding line of work." She fidgets with her coaster, not meeting my eyes, but I'm captivated by the way her eyelashes lie soft and dark along the top of her cheekbones. So pretty. Then she looks up and I'm caught staring. A flush warms my cheeks as she continues, "I mean, I help people, and that's cool, but you change their lives."

"Some of them. Did you always want to be a plumber?"

Shaking her head, she laughs. "Hell no. I wanted to be an *equestrian*." She says it with a childish lisp and makes air quotes around the word. "Does anyone *want* to snake out drains for a living? Like I said, Dad taught me. It's good money, and I don't have to work for anyone else. It's what it is, you know?"

"You get along well with him? Your dad?"

"Oh totally. It's like . . . you wouldn't expect this big redneck dude to be okay with the gay, but he's cool. And I was always a bit of a daddy's girl, following him around, wearing my pink glittery toy tool belt and pretending I could fix anything. And he never told me I couldn't. He did have to break it to me gently that we couldn't afford a horse though." She says it without bitterness, smiling like even that is a happy memory.

"He sounds great."

"He is. How about your family—you said you're divorced? How long has that been?"

Butterflies in my stomach. How much to tell?

"Um, yeah, my family's okay. We've been through some rough patches, and I—" My face grows hot, and I grip my beer in both hands like it's a lifeline. "I'm sorry, the divorce is hard to talk about."

"Are you okay?" Her eyes go wide with concern. "I'm sorry, I didn't mean to pry, just making small talk. I was wondering if your interest was a rebound thing. Which if it is—"

"It's not that. I still have a lot of complicated feelings for my ex, but she isn't . . . she isn't queer."

Joe's forehead wrinkles in confusion, and then her lips fall open in a little round *O*. She looks at me, studying me as if trying to see signs of who I used to be, or maybe still puzzling out what I told her. Finally, she smiles. "Thank you for trusting me—I can't imagine coming out is easy."

Relief floods me and frees up the words I'd been struggling to say.

"It's why talking about the divorce is hard. It's why talking about my family is hard. It's not that any of them are awful or anything— even my dickhead brother manages the right pronouns most of the time—it's just . . ." Oh God. My nose is stinging. I can't cry here. Not fucking now. "It's complicated, and it ends up being easier if we don't see each other much. Holidays, if we're all in town."

"I get it. I'm sorry." She takes my hand in hers and gives it a gentle squeeze. The contact is electric, bringing me back to the present and the attraction and the first-date excitement. "Remembering your pronouns is, like, the bare minimum of courtesy, even for dickhead brothers. I guess small talk can be a minefield for you, huh?"

I take a deep breath. "I don't think there's such a thing as small talk when you're getting to know someone. Everything is a revelation."

Her smile breaks out then, a revelation in itself, and she nods. "Totally."

Stella returns with our food and slides into the booth next to me after setting it on the table. She leans toward me and whispers conspiratorially "She giving you the pitch yet?"

"Pitch?" I look at Joe quizzically.

Her grin fades. "Yeah. Okay, here is where I confess that I didn't just invite you out because I think you're cute. I totally do. But I kind of had an ulterior motive."

My heart sinks. The first woman I've actually been interested in since Lisa moved out, and she comes with ulterior motives. "I see."

"Shit. I'm sorry." Stella stands up. "Okay, I'm gonna go." She flashes an apologetic smile and returns to her perch behind the bar.

"Hear me out, okay?" Joe points to a banner over the bar. "See that?"

*Lake Lovelace Rollergirls.* The banner is purple and silver, with retro lettering, stars, and hearts.

"Yeah?"

"I founded the team—I coach them now. Stella's our jammer."

"What does that have to do with me?"

"You ever roller-skate when you were a kid?"

"I was born in 1977; what do you think?"

She grins. "Okay, so, we're a new team, we don't have a lot of members, and we're trying to change that. The competitive season runs from December to June, but this year's season was a total bust. We need talent. You're a former professional athlete. You're strong, and if you wakeboarded professionally, you've got to have good balance. Also, you know how to compete."

Hope flares up in me. I've missed competition so much. Does she know what she's dangling in front of me? Is she really asking?

"You want me to play on your team?"

"I want you to try out—I can't promise anything. Before you skate in a bout, you have to pass some tests, but yeah. I want you to skate for us. I'd love to have you on the team."

"This is the pitch Stella was talking about?"

Joe grins. "Yeah."

"Before I say yes—is it going to be a problem that I'm trans?"

She sets down her glass and meets my gaze dead-on, unflinching. "No. If anyone on the team has a problem with a trans woman skating for us, they know where to find the door. Derby is for everyone."

"You believe that?" I don't know where the sudden rush of anger comes from. "You'd really let your established skaters go for me?"

She shrugs. "I'm going to be honest; I don't think it's gonna be a problem. But yeah, I would. And if I'm wrong, and it is a problem, then I'm on your side. Just because I've known them longer doesn't mean I want bigots on my team."

I swallow the sudden lump in my throat.

"So, you're the coach. Stella's the jammer." I make a mental note to google the term online later. "And you want me to skate."

"Yes."

"So, this isn't a date, is it?" Disappointment tempers my excitement at the prospect of team sports.

She flinches now. "I'm sorry. I like you, but if you skate for us . . ." She glances over to Stella. "It could be a problem if I dated you. But a few of us on the team are queer and we're all pretty close. We hang out here or go to the gay bar together. I'd like to be friends, you know?"

If I want to date her—she hasn't said she isn't interested in dating, only that it could be a problem—I can't skate for them. And she's already made it clear that she wants me to try out. Which means she probably doesn't want to date me more than she wants me to skate. But it's not just skating, she's offering, it's a fellowship with other women. Women like me, queer women—that sounds like the kind of friendship sorely missing from my life. Not that Ben and Eddie aren't the absolute *best*—but sometimes a girl wants the companionship of other girls. As for the rest of it? Competition and a dangerous sport? I'm all over that.

"I'll try out." A thrill runs down my arms, and I can't hold back a smile. But even though I'm glad, and I'm full of anticipation, a small part of me feels a pang of what might have been.

"I'll send you some YouTube videos first, okay? And you can call me or text or whatever if you change your mind." She grins and shakes her head. "I'm so excited—we're in the middle of a recruitment cycle right now, but depending on your skills we can probably get you up to speed with the rest of the fresh meat."

"Fresh meat?" I raise an eyebrow at her.

"Derby talk. You'll get used to it." Her grin falls a bit. "I mean—I guess I'm taking that for granted. I hope you'll like it. I've got a good feeling."

Our small talk moves to other subjects, safe subjects, as we finish our beers and order another round. I'm relieved to find out that the rasp in her voice isn't from smoking, but from paralysis in one of her vocal cords after a childhood infection.

"Yeah, I've been talking like a pack-a-day smoker since I was six!" She laughs. "It used to bother me, back in school. But now I like how distinctive it is. No one else sounds like me. No yelling for me though, no loud cheering at the bouts. Can't risk the damage."

Too soon, the second round is finished, and even though I can't drag my eyes away from her lips, her smile, the weird-huge spark between us, I also know I have a client at 5:30 a.m. and so we close out our tab—which she insists on paying—and then she walks me to my car. She slides her hand into mine, casual and easy.

"You aren't on the team yet," she whispers, backing me up against my car, her hips hitting mine. The closeness of her, the scent of her skin, and the cocky little smile are a sudden, sharp turn-on.

Fuck roller derby.

I lean in as she rises on tiptoe and presses her lips to mine. A perfect fit. If the connection between us so far has been sparks, her kiss is an inferno.

One of my hands slides down to her waist; the other buries itself in her hair. She whimpers into my mouth, and I had forgotten—it's been so long, so fucking long since I've shared a first kiss with someone, and she feels so good. Her hand slides up from my waist to my breast, cupping me through the lace of my pushup bra. My whole body goes hot and heavy at once as her thumb circles, brushes, and circles again over my nipple.

I lower my face to that sweet, spicy-smelling place where her neck meets shoulder, and I nip right there on salty skin.

"Damn, girl." She mumbles against my lips, but her thumb keeps teasing, rolling my nipple between it and a forefinger.

I drop my head against the car and take in a deep breath to clear my mind and calm my racing heart.

"I should go," I murmur, but then I take another plucking kiss, which leads to a bite on my earlobe and her leg thrust between mine, pressing into me and making me arch, craving friction and closeness.

Her lips trace from my ear down my neck; goose bumps erupt along my skin, and I shudder against her. I can't remember the last time I've been this turned on.

"Joe," I whisper. "We're in the parking lot."

A low laugh rumbles out of her as she pulls back, her short hair all rumpled and sexy looking. "And you have an early client."

"Yeah." I push down the swell of regret. "And if I'm going to skate on your team . . ."

She flinches, her swagger falling away and a pinched look coming to her eyes. "We probably shouldn't—"

"You're sexy as hell." I blurt it out, wishing I had it in me to play it cool, but I never have; I've always been a heart on my sleeve kind of girl. "But I just got divorced and I shouldn't get involved in something complicated right now."

She nods. "I'm sorry. If it makes you feel better, I wish Stella had kept her mouth shut and I'd never mentioned derby. I'd be setting the alarm on my bedside table to wake you up for your early client." There's a new teasing smile in her voice.

"Well, maybe I'll suck at skating." I offer, and we both laugh.

"Do you really want to do it?"

"Yeah. I think I really do."

"Come here." She pulls me into a quick hug, letting go almost as fast as she grabs me, then she takes a few steps back. "I'm so glad. I'll send you videos, okay?"

"Sounds great." I give her a little wave. "We'll talk soon."

I admire the easy sway of her hips as she crosses the parking lot to her van. She looks over her shoulder once and smiles sweetly. Is she feeling this bittersweet tug-of-war too? When she turns back, I unlock my car and climb inside. I'm halfway home before I realize I'm humming "Suspicious Minds."

# chapter FOUR

**I**'m sitting on the hood of my car outside Reed's Gym at quarter after five the next morning, iced coffee in hand, when Nate Reed pulls up next to me and rolls down his window, his face still red from his 4 a.m. run.

"Durham, you got a client coming in?"

Nate's one of those gruff ex-military guys who calls everyone by their last names. At first, I found it off-putting, but then I saw how some of the clients responded to it, like it gave them that little bit of oomph they needed to grind out that last rep. Now I'm used to it, though I still wish he'd call me Tina.

"Jeremy. He's got a competition coming up."

Nate grunts and cuts his car engine. "Another one? What kind of schedule do you have him on? Kid's got more muscles than sense. Stay on him about not overtraining."

Bitterness washes through me. Nate never used to question me about training schedules. I'm a damn good trainer, and I've been working with Jeremy for years. Yes, he got an overtraining injury and missed a competition last year, but that was because the stubborn kid started training for a marathon without telling me and without adjusting his lifting schedule, not because I hadn't been doing my job.

"Right," I grit out, fighting the urge to flip Nate the bird. I need this job, and no matter how casual and laid-back my work environment is, some lines you don't cross.

I follow Nate, a great hulk of grumbling and muscle, as he makes his way to the front door. He holds it open for me and smiles. It softens his ruddy face, transforming him from the hardened Marine to the favorite uncle I never had.

"You look pretty today. You do something different with your hair?"

A blush heats my face as I brush past him and finger the end of my ponytail. "No, I don't think so. It needs a trim."

He shakes his head. "Maybe it's the makeup. New . . . shit, I don't know what any of that stuff is called. You look good, Durham. Take the fucking compliment."

"Yes, sir." I laugh, forgiving him—a little—for the crack about Jeremy's training. "Thanks."

Jeremy arrives right on time. I catch a glimpse of him out the windows, jogging up to the gym, pouring sweat already. He's in his early twenties and all of five feet seven inches, a bundle of wild energy and humor, grinning as he comes through the door and shivers at the touch of the air conditioning. We don't keep it really cold or anything, but a summer morning in Lake Lovelace is like a sauna—and even the slightest amount of air conditioning feels icy.

We take a few minutes to talk over where he's at in his training, whether he has any unusual aches or pains. He swings his left elbow in a circle.

"Little bit, in this shoulder." He gestures with his chin and then looks up at me. "It's tight in the mornings, and I had a twinge when I was working my traps last week."

"Did you ice it?"

He grins at me, ducking his head. "Twenty minutes, every eight hours, and I took ibuprofen too, but not before coming in. Even though it's leg day."

"Good. All right, let's get started."

Jeremy is one of those clients I mostly spot and advise—I don't do his workout with him like I might with a newbie. In theory, he knows what he's doing. He should be in great shape for his competition, but when his legs start shaking halfway through his squats, I call a stop. Goddamn it.

"Have you eaten today?"

He shakes his head. "I'll grab a shake after my workout."

"Jeremy." I try to make my voice gentle, but it comes out with an edge to it.

He hangs his head like a scolded puppy, then his words spill from him in a defensive tumble.

"I don't have an eating disorder or anything. I just wanted to get a run in before the workout, and I didn't have time for both."

"Dude." I start moving the weights back to the rack. "Defensive much? The fact that you went straight to 'eating disorder' should concern you. You cannot—*cannot*—maintain this kind of schedule without adequate food. You aren't giving your muscles the fuel they need to make it through these workouts. And don't tell me you had an energy drink like that's enough. Energy supplements are made of caffeine and God-knows-what. You know better. And Jer—" I put my hand on his shoulder and he looks up "—I'm not going to train you if you don't eat."

His body tightens. "You can't stop training me."

I flinch away from the hint of menace in his voice. "Calm down, please."

"I'm not—" He glances down at his clenched fists, then loosens them. "I promise I'll do better with the eating."

"Skip the run before you skip the meal."

"I'll try." He scrubs a hand across his face.

"I'm serious, Jeremy, I won't train you if you're not eating. It's dangerous."

"Are you firing me as a client?"

Am I? Jesus, I hadn't thought that far ahead. I can't exactly afford to fire any clients right now. And I don't think Nate can afford for me to fire anyone either. He hasn't said anything, but an empty gym speaks for itself. But beyond that—this is Jeremy. My five thirty workout buddy. Literally the reason I get up in the mornings.

"No. But you're done for today. I've got some bananas and peanut butter in the lunch room, and orange juice. Before you run home, you need to eat something."

He wrinkles up his nose. "Juice has a lot of sugar in it."

Rolling my eyes, I start toward the kitchen, calling over my shoulder, "And you have about three percent body fat. You need sugar—and protein. And fat. It's called fuel for those muscles you work so hard."

In the kitchen, I lean against the fridge and try to collect myself. Should I tell Nate? He's going to want to know if we're in danger of losing a client. Can I even help Jeremy? I rack my brain, trying to think what I know of his family life. He has—had?—a girlfriend. What's her name? Emma? Emily?

I spread the peanut butter on a piece of whole wheat bread, grab a banana, and pour a bit of juice in a cup. As if for a freaking child. The boy needs more than a trainer—he needs a keeper. Shaking my head, I make my way back to the free-weight area.

And he's gone. His bag is gone. His towel is gone. He's gone.

*Fuck.*

"Hey, did you see Jeremy leave?" I pop my head into Nate's office, where he's hunched over a computer, pecking at the keys with two fingers.

"No—is he done already?"

"I cut his workout short because he was shaking. Working out on an empty stomach. I went to get him some carbs and he disappeared."

Nate crosses his arms over his chest and sits back in his chair.

"Disappeared?"

"Yeah. I mean, it was so totally awkward. I told him I wasn't going to train him if he didn't eat, and he completely overreacted, talking about eating disorders—super defensive." I repeat our conversation to Nate, whose face grows grimmer and grimmer.

"That fucking kid." He shakes his head. "All right, call him later to check on him, but trust your gut. Eating disorders are nothing to mess around with. And if he's dealing with that kind of shit, he needs real help. I've got brochures somewhere."

"Brochures?" I'd laugh if it weren't so serious. "You think the kid's gonna stop restricting calories because of a brochure?"

Nate shrugs. "It's not like we can afford to hire a nutritionist. And we can't afford to lose a client either. Jesus. We're barely keeping the lights on. I mean, obviously the kid's health is the important thing, but . . ."

"What about summer memberships? Beat the heat specials?"

"We saw an uptick in those last month, but they've leveled off. People seem to be getting their exercise somewhere else this summer.

I knew we shouldn't have done that two-years-up-front promotion for New Year's. We aren't getting the recurring payments we need."

I slump back against the doorjamb and stare at him. "So what are you saying? We're going under?"

"I'm saying, get that boy in here, working out and winning competitions where other vain muscle-heads can see our name on his T-shirt."

He digs a pile of brochures out of his desk drawer and tosses them on the paper-littered desk. "And see if there's anything in there he can use."

I pick up the brochures, not that they'll do Jeremy any good if he won't read them. A sinking, sick feeling twists through my gut.

The next night, Elvis and I curl up on the couch with my laptop, and I pull up the YouTube videos Joe sent me. Familiar gym-sounds fill the room: squeaks and people moving, and murmurs around whoever was taking the video. Blurring and shaking slightly, it focuses in on the action below.

A sea of black and yellow helmets and elbows flying. At first, it doesn't look like much is happening—a group of women shoving at each other, the occasional shout, but mostly a mass of bodies pushing. But then I see it—the breakthrough moment when the woman in black with a star on her helmet grabs the hips of one of her teammates, ducks low, and pulls. She shoots past her teammate and takes off like a shot as the crowd shouts and whistles.

The video ends.

That's what Joe wanted me to see. But why? I watch it again. Watch the struggle, the maneuvering. Now that I know what the end goal was, I can see the subtle shifts and the way the teammates work together to hold back the girls with the stars on their helmets. I pull out my phone.

*The stars?*

I queue up the next video while I wait for an answer.

*Jammers. They score points by lapping members of the other team.*

I watch a few more, enjoying the technique, the fast skating, the way the girls all seem to light up as they fly across the track. Occasionally, I text Joe, clarifying the things I see on the screen, what they mean, why she wanted me to see them.

The last video shows a bout in full swing, ending in a terrible crash and one girl being led off the track, hobbling, to the applause of the crowd.

*Is this one supposed to show me how seriously I could get hurt?*

I can almost hear her low, sexy laugh.

*Nah, you're a grown-up, you can figure out that stuff on your own. You see what happened there? The first girl who fell, she sort of sprawled out, and everyone else fell too?*

I watch it again up until that point.

*Yeah.*

I replay the fall, seeing the moment the first of the other girls trips.

*Derby is a team game. You gotta tuck up, fall small. Don't bring anyone else down. Skating fast and kicking ass is fun, but there's more to it than that. It's working together, not falling together.*

I don't have a lot of experience with team sports. Wakeboarding wasn't like that. Even with the companionship on the boat, a big part of what made it special was being alone at the end of that rope, demanding the laws of physics lift you up like a god. It was all about the individual glory.

But in spite of my unfamiliarity with the dynamic, I get the message. She's sent me a half-dozen videos with one idea in mind: teamwork. Not as a lecture—I barely know her, but I know that isn't her MO. This is a reminder of what she's promising—companionship, friendship. Teamwork. Something bigger than individual glory.

And damn, I want it.

*You really love it, don't you?*

She doesn't reply right away, but when she does, it isn't what I expected.

*You will too. I have a good feeling. Text me your shoe size so I can borrow some skates for you, okay?*

I snuggle a little closer to Elvis and watch the last video.

# chapter FIVE

I call Jeremy from the parking lot of the Lake Lovelace State University gym.

"Hello?"

"It's Tina, from Reed's. How are you doing?"

The line is silent for a long moment, then he sighs heavily.

"I'm sorry, Tina. I shouldn't have left like I did. I was embarrassed about getting mad, and I panicked a little, I guess."

"Are you coming in tomorrow?"

"Yeah. And I'll eat first. I promise."

"Jeremy, if you need help—"

"Just forget it. I was stupid. It won't happen again." He hangs up, leaving me to stare at my phone. That could have gone better, but I guess it could have been worse too.

I tuck my phone into my handbag and look around. A few minivans and old SUVs haunt the mostly empty parking lot. Joe's van is off to one side, so I know I'm in the right place.

I don't know why I was expecting a roller-skating rink, but I guess it makes sense that they wouldn't close their doors on a lucrative evening skate time so the roller derby team could have tryouts. Or whatever these are. Joe said they were in the middle of a recruitment cycle.

The gym smells like sweat, and the sounds of skates and voices echo off the cinder-block walls. My gut wrenches a little with nerves, but then I see her. Back in her beater and cutoffs, Joe is talking to Stella in a corner, making big gestures and laughing. When she spots me, she waves and starts skating over.

VANESSA NORTH

"Hey." She comes to a neat stop in front of me. "I have skates for you. I borrowed them from Katie's rink." She leads me to the bleachers, moving as easily on skates as she does without them. Reaching into a black bag, she pulls out ugly brown rental skates with purple laces. "You'll want to buy your own if you decide this is your thing, but until then . . . here. I, um—" she looks away, biting her lip "—I put new laces in them, 'cause the laces on rentals are always shitty."

I take the skates with a lump in my throat, nodding gratefully, and then I sit down and pull them on. It's been a long time since I've put on a pair of roller skates. Maybe not since high school, when Lisa and I used to actually date. I stand up and give an experimental turn. Yeah, you don't lose it, do you?

Joe watches me, a grin on her face. "Been awhile?"

"Yeah."

"Can you skate backward?"

I learned how once. How did that work? I bend my knees, look behind me to make sure the way is clear, then push out with first one foot, then the other, propelling myself back a few yards before braking. Hell yeah. I grin up at Joe, who returns my grin.

"I guess you can. Did you come straight from work? Do you need to warm up?"

"I did come straight from work, but I do paperwork at the end of the day. Maybe I should take a few laps to loosen my muscles."

"Sure, I'll do them with you, get a feel for your technique."

We set off at an easy pace, and she slips into a natural teacher mode that reminds me of Ben. "See those girls over there?" She points to a group gathered around Stella. "They're learning how to fall safely—minimizing the chances of injury to themselves or others."

"Do people get hurt a lot?"

"We've been mostly injury-free so far—Katie sprained an ankle at the beginning of the season and had to sit the rest of it out, but that's the only one so far. We take safety pretty seriously."

As we round the corner into our second lap, she starts to pick up the pace. "Do you have any questions about how the game is played?"

I've been studying. "Let me see if I've got this: each team has five players on the track. Three blockers, a jammer—who tries to get past the blockers so she can lap them and score points for each one she passes—and a pivot, who is a blocker but can strategically become the jammer if the star covering the helmet—"

"The panty," Joe supplies.

"—if the panty is successfully passed from the jammer to the pivot."

"That's the gist, yeah." Joe grins at me. "What else?"

"The scoring period is called the jam, and it lasts two minutes, but the lead jammer can strategically call it off early by putting her hands on her hips."

"That's right, good. You warmed up yet? Ready to show me what you got?"

"Hell yeah."

"Okay, so you see those cones over there?"

Across the gym, a miniature obstacle course has been set up: orange traffic cones, a few sacks of sand. I nod.

"Grab a helmet, wrist guards, and pads from the blue bag by Stella—you'll want to get your own, but we always have a couple extras of the safety gear in case someone forgets something. I want you to build up a little speed, then weave around the cones in figure eights two times. And if you can, I wanna see you jump the sack at the end of the row."

Jump the sack? Holy shit. Can I do that? How do you jump in roller skates?

"Why the jump?"

"If someone falls in front of you and you can't get around them, what do you do?" She shrugs. "You could crash into them, but that would suck for both of you."

"Got it." I pull on the unfamiliar safety gear, then push down the flutter of nerves as I skate over to the cones, picking up speed along the way. The weight of the skates is strange on my feet as I go into the first turn, but I push through the unfamiliar feeling and cross one foot over the other, building speed on the cross between turns. After the second figure eight, I skate straight toward the sacks, determined to jump.

Panic hits me like a freight train.

I can see myself sprawled on the ground, bones broken. *Hell no.* At the last minute, I swerve around it. I put my hands on my hips and try to shake it off. I look up at Joe, expecting to see disappointment on her face, but she's grinning and clapping her wrist guards together.

"That was awesome. You nailed those figure eights, and you were fast. Really great work, T."

Stella skates over and points at the sack. "You want some tips on how to jump that?"

"Maybe? I panicked. I think I can do it. I mean, it's like doing an ollie on water, right?"

She cocks her head to one side, studying me.

"I've never done an ollie on water, but yeah, I imagine so." She turns toward the cones and does her own set of figure eights, coming straight at me—no, the sacks—out of the final turn. I watch her approach them, watch how she gets her butt low and then picks up her feet and soars over the sacks. Feet down, she turns and hauls ass back into the figure eights.

Holy shit, the girl can skate. But Joe had led me to believe the team wasn't very good? How on earth does she expect me to keep up?

Another girl approaches me, not as smoothly as Stella or Joe, but with a confidence I don't have yet. "Hi, I'm Lauren."

"Tina."

"You fresh meat too?"

I wince. "Yeah."

"You were really fast. Where'd you learn to skate like that? I feel like I'm always going to be stuck on the basics."

"I always liked to move fast. Back when I was a pro wakeboarder, we'd get the speed way up on the boat so we could fly behind it."

"Damn. So you get the balance stuff too. Lucky you. I sometimes wonder if I only wanted to do this for an excuse to wear fishnets."

I glance down at her legs. Sure enough, she's wearing ripped-up black fishnets. She's cute and curvy, round all over, but she's tugging self-consciously at the hem of her shorts. Maybe she isn't totally comfortable with the look.

"They suit you."

She blushes. "Thanks. Okay. Gonna go through the obstacle course myself now."

I watch as she moves through the pattern, doing all the right stuff with her feet, but not committing to the speed. Her eyes widen every time she crosses one foot over the other, like she's just impressed herself at her ability to do that.

"Butt down, Lou," Stella calls out to her, and Lauren squats a little lower, but wobbles, and one of her skates scoots forward. I wince as she goes down hard on her butt. I don't think that's what Stella meant.

"You okay?" I skate over and help her up.

"Yeah, I'm fine. Plenty of padding." She pats her backside for emphasis. "I'm not the most coordinated. I don't know why I thought derby would be a good idea. Chase laughed when I told him I was going to try out. God, this is stupid. But I'm not going to let him be right about it."

Her face settles in determination.

"Who's Chase?"

"My husband." She swallows. "I'm not going to make excuses for him—he's usually a sweetheart, but he's being a dick about this. He doesn't think I can do it because I'm fat. I can't help being a big girl—"

*What the hell?* What kind of asshole makes his wife feel bad about her weight *and* about exercising?

"He gives you shit about your weight? And about playing a sport?"

Shrugging, she adjusts her helmet. "It's complicated. He likes my body fine, if you know what I mean. I think he's more pissed about me leaving the kids with him so I can skate, and he's lashing out at a sore spot for both of us."

When I don't say anything, she explains, "He used to be a football player in high school, so there's a jealousy thing. Meanwhile I grew up thinking sports were just for skinny girls. But this is something *I* can do—and maybe do well. I don't know."

The determined set of her jaw and the steel behind her eyes make me believe she's not only going to do it, but she's going to kick ass too.

"Good for you."

"All right, ladies." Joe claps her hands a few times over her head, skating into the middle of the gym. She keeps her voice down, but everyone quiets to listen to her. "I think everyone is here now, so we're going to get started with assessments—tryouts, for the fresh meat. Let's start with 27/5. The goal is to do twenty-seven laps in five minutes or under. Some pointers—get low, build speed in the straightaways, and stay to the inside of the corners. Tina, I want you to participate even though this is your first time. It'll give you a good idea where you stand."

"Oh, man. I thought we weren't doing this until next week." Lauren bites at her lip, her eyes a little glassy. "I'm not ready."

"Ready? It's just straight-up skating, right?" I bump her shoulder with my own. "You can do that."

"Yeah, but it's skating *fast*. I've been working on skating *better*. I passed everything else already, but the 27/5 is—" she shakes her head "—it's the last thing I need to pass to make the team."

Oh. I've seen this before, this nervousness. I used to see it with other riders on the wake boat. *Performance anxiety.* "Hey, if you've been working on technique, won't speed come along with that?"

She wipes at her eyes, then looks over at me. "Maybe. I just didn't think it was going to be today. I thought I'd have more time, and I just— I want Chase and the kids to get to see me skate in a bout."

"Okay, so let's focus on that. Imagine you're skating in your first bout. You're about to skate as clean and as fast as you can. Chase and the kids are there to watch. What are their names?"

"Kaylee and Braden."

"Okay, Chase and Kaylee and Braden are all there to watch. Little Kaylee is going to see her mom kick butt. Braden is wide-eyed with excitement. And Chase is so proud of you, he could burst. That's what I want you to think about when you go out there and skate. And seriously, what's the worst that could happen? You fall down? So the fuck what? People fall down."

Lauren shakes her head and smiles at me. "You're really good at this pep-talking stuff."

Of all the things I've been good at in my life—wakeboarding, weight lifting—that might be the one I'm proudest of. "You'll do great."

And she does. She's not the fastest skater, but I can see in her eyes how bad she wants this, and while it takes her precious seconds to build up speed, a sort of calm settles over her, and she flies out of the final turn with a fierce determination on her face.

When Joe calls out Lauren's time, I expect her to cheer or shout for joy, but she surprises me by bursting into tears and clinging to me, both arms around my waist. Yeah, I've seen this before too. At marathon finish lines and double-up contests, when someone wants their body to do something so bad, they don't let themselves believe it can. When they finally nail it, something like a storm of grief hits them. Whether for their old doubts, or for the belief they never let themselves have, I don't know.

I hold her and make some shushing noises while she cries out her relief and joy, and everything Joe said about teamwork and companionship hits home so hard, I start tearing up too. And I just freaking met this girl.

Joe skates over to us and joins in the hug, sandwiching Lauren between us. "You did it, Lauren! I'm so fucking proud of you. Time to pick out your derby name, baby." She meets my gaze over Lauren's shoulder. "You ready?"

A grin spreads across my face. "Let's do it."

I don't make the team.

I didn't expect to—it's only my first day. But I still feel a twinge of sadness as I watch the others celebrating with Lauren, a longing to be a part of their celebration. A handful of other girls didn't pass the assessments either. My downfall was the jump, which is pretty fucking humiliating for a wakeboarder, but I chickened out. Falling on a hard gym floor, no matter what I said to Lauren, is a lot scarier than falling on water.

"You did really well." Joe appears at my side as I unbuckle my borrowed helmet and grimace. How many other sweaty heads have been in there?

"Thanks." I glance over at her, and I can't help but think that she looks pretty with her cheeks flushed and her hair damp with sweat. *Stop fantasizing about the coach, T.*

"I mean it. I bet you could pass all the assessments with a few weeks' hard work. I mean, if that's what you want. I guess this was a trial for us too." She bites her lip and peers up at me. "Did we pass?"

A laugh bubbles up in my chest, and I nod. "Yeah. I had a great time."

"Awesome." She hugs me then, a quick, self-conscious thing. Is she remembering our gropey kiss in the parking lot the other night? "Listen, it's sort of a tradition. When new girls make the team and pick out their derby names, we all go to Blue's and have a few drinks to celebrate. You're totally welcome to come. We're meeting over there in about an hour to give folks time to go home and shower if they want."

"I'd like that, but . . ." I look down at the skates she brought for me to wear and feel like an ass, declining her invitation. "Elvis."

She shrugs. "Bring him along; Stella's boss won't care. He can be our unofficial mascot."

"Really?"

"Yeah, really. These girls are going to *love* him."

I run into the house, dump a cup and a half of food into Elvis's bowl, and book it down the hall to the bathroom. Somehow, I manage to shower and blow-dry my hair in record time, do the bare minimum of makeup—it'll be dark in the bar, right?—and then fall into a complete panic over my wardrobe.

Seriously, it's a million degrees outside—what says "I want you to think I'm sexy and not at all interested in dating you even though I totally am and still manages to pass the "July evening in Florida" test?

Rejecting my skinny jeans—too hot—a sundress—too much leg!—and shorts—ew, I look like my *mom*—I finally settle on a halter maxi dress. The bright pink hibiscus flowers say "festive and casual," and the halter gives my décolletage a little extra something. And, unlike the shorter dress, I don't feel like I'm showing an obscene amount of leg when I wear it. I slip on some fancy flat sandals and grab Elvis's leash, giving it a jingle.

He comes running, but stops dead when he realizes I'm dressed to go out. Whining, he lies on the floor at my feet and shows me his belly.

"You're stupidly adorable." I bend over and scratch the proffered pudge. "Come on, you're coming with me."

If there is one thing Elvis loves, it's riding in the car with the window down and his ears flopping in the breeze. He hangs his tongue out and grunts with joy as I drive to the bar, arriving only a few minutes late. I pull into the parking space next to Joe's van and roll up the windows before cutting the engine.

As Elvis and I make our way to the front door, I catch sight of Lauren out front, her phone to her ear and a pained expression on her face.

"Heat up some leftovers and give the kids the Kraft macaroni. No. Come on, you can cook it in the microwave. You don't need me to make mac and cheese."

When she sees me, a grim expression falls across her face and her voice tightens. "Chase, I'm going to hang up now. I'll be home in a couple hours. Good night."

I can hear her husband bellowing on the other end of the line until it's cut short.

"Hey," I greet her.

"Sorry." She shrugs and holds up her phone. "God, he's such a jerk about derby. He congratulated me and then whined over having to feed the kids. His own fucking kids, for fuck's sake."

"Don't let him rain on your parade. This is Elvis, by the way."

She looks down at my goofy-faced dog and grins. "He's awesome."

"He really is. Let's go in, yeah?"

Out of years of habit, I open the door and hold it wide for her. She thanks me, and I follow her inside, to where Joe is holding court over several tables pushed together in the back. She's wearing her beater and camo cutoffs, and her dark hair flops in front of her eyes, all sexy.

Even though Stella isn't working, she's behind the bar, filling a pitcher. She grins and waves at me as we sit down, and without spilling a drop, turns off the tap and starts filling a pint glass with water.

"For the dog." She holds it up and smiles. "He's *so* cute!"

And just like that, Elvis and I are the center of attention. Joe comes around the table to hug me and scratch his ears, and he flops onto his back to receive the adoration of the whole team.

"Tina!" Stella comes over and sits down beside me, placing the pitcher on the table and the pint glass on the floor for Elvis. "You were fantastic. So fast. Fearless. We'll get you jumping in no time, I promise."

"Thanks, Stell." I reach for a plastic cup on the table and fill it from the pitcher. "I hope so."

"No joke, you were amazing. I still can't believe it's your first day. You weren't even wearing derby skates!" Lauren pipes up, holding out her own cup to be filled. She's still wearing her fishnets, but her hair is falling in big gold curls around her shoulders. I fill her cup and give one of those ringlets a little tug.

"Nope, *you* were amazing. Congratulations again."

"Have you thought of a name yet?" Stella throws an arm around Lauren and pulls her into a sideways hug.

"Yeah, um, I think it's going to be Lau-Rayna Terror."

"Nice." Joe raises her glass. "To Lau-Rayna Terror!" The cheer goes up, and we all join in, laughing and clapping as Lauren blushes.

About a half hour later, Lauren takes another call, heading outside with her phone pressed to her ear and a fake smile plastered on her face. I notice Joe following her with her eyes, frowning.

"I'm worried about her," I say softly, and Joe meets my gaze with a sharp look.

"Yeah, me too. Her husband isn't handling her playing derby well."

"You know her outside of this?"

"I know *him*. He's actually a good friend who contracts for me sometimes."

Well, that puts a different spin on things. Knowing he's friends with Joe makes it harder for me to make him the villain in this story.

"He's a plumber?"

"Jack of all trades—plumber, electrician. General handyman shit. He's not really that big of an asshole. I don't know what's going on between the two of them, if he's jealous of the time she's spending out of the house or what. I never would have suggested she play derby if I'd realized it would strain their marriage. It seemed like a good idea in the moment."

After seeing Lauren sob with relief when she made the team, I couldn't imagine her not having derby. "No, she needs this. She's getting something positive out of it—you saw how happy she was tonight."

Joe smiles, but it doesn't reach her eyes. "I feel guilty though. Like I'm causing trouble."

"But maybe the trouble—the shake-up in their lives—can help them both. I see it a lot with my clients, the strain on a relationship when one partner decides to make a change in their life. The other feels like they're being left behind. But they need to figure out how to work through it together."

"You know, I never thought of it that way. I bet Chase *is* feeling left behind. How do they fix it?"

Shrugging, I take another sip of my warming beer. "Communication. Finding common ground. Some don't ever fix it— my wife and I didn't. Some come back stronger than ever. You know Chase and Lauren better than I do. You think they're going to pull through?"

"Chase isn't exactly the spill-his-guts kind of guy. But common ground—there's no reason he can't get involved too. Hell, the kids can come skate around while she practices. I'm gonna go talk to her. Mind if I take Elvis for a walk? You know, for an excuse to be outside when she hangs up?"

"Of course."

"It means a lot, you trusting me with your dog." She leans in and gives me a little peck on the cheek. "I'll bring him back in a few."

I hand over his rhinestone-studded leash and watch her lead him outside, a funny ache in my chest. It's easy to fall for someone who fixes things. Lisa always had solutions and strategies and plans to make things better. Something about the way Joe wants people to be happy, the way she goes about seeing that everyone is taken care of? It would be far too easy to find myself depending on someone like that all over again.

# chapter SIX

july gives way to August with a lurch as I make room for derby in my life. I've been a professional athlete, and I've worked as a personal trainer for years now, so my body is no stranger to the aches and pains of hard work. I take a strange comfort in my sore and exhausted muscles every morning, and a perverse pride in the bruises covering my legs and ass. I earned every fucking one of them trying to jump over that stupid sand sack.

Jeremy and I achieve a measure of detente after our confrontation. He keeps coming in first thing in the morning with the dregs of a protein drink in his hand. I don't know for sure that he's actually consuming them, but he's not shaking when he works out, and he's maintaining his weight—maybe even gaining, which is what I like to see with my weight lifters.

Nate, on the other hand, is getting more and more distressed over the lack of gym traffic. He corners me in the lunchroom one afternoon in early August.

"Durham, you got any leads on new training clients?"

I pause, a forkful of salad halfway to my mouth. "Um . . ."

"Sorry, I know you're having lunch, but I'm trying to come up with ideas for getting people in here. What if I gave you a commission on new clients you bring in?"

If that salad had been in my mouth, I'd have choked on it. "I'm not a sales person."

"Desperate times, Durham." He gives me a speculative look. "How about those girls you skate with? Any of them interested in a discounted personal training package?"

"I dunno, Nate. You got any brochures?"

He grins at me. "If I get some made up, will you hand 'em out?"

"Don't waste the money on printing. Put a status on the gym's Facebook page proclaiming our support for the Lake Lovelace Rollergirls and include a coupon code for training packages. I'll ask Joe to share it on the team's page, and we'll see what shakes out."

Nate stares at me for a minute, eyebrows climbing his forehead. "Well, okay. You're not bad at this, you know."

"I'm still not a salesperson."

"Guess I don't have to pay you a bonus when your brilliant marketing strategy pans out."

"Just keep me employed. I need this job."

The second weekend in August is a big scrimmage with some of the other teams in central Florida. Out of season, it's not an officially sanctioned game, so it won't count toward division seeding. Still, as we pile into two minivans at 5 a.m., we're buzzing with giddy anticipation. I'm not playing—I haven't passed the assessments yet—but I ride along, every bit as eager to see my first bout as Lauren is to skate in hers.

Lauren sits next to me and bubbles on about homeschooling her kids. Stella, who it turns out is in the final semester of her senior year at LLSU, cuddles in the back with Rebecca, the raven-haired tattoo artist responsible for Joe's sleeve. I hear them murmuring for a while, then they fall quiet. When I peek over my shoulder, they're both asleep, heads together between them. Joe drives, her eyes hidden behind dark sunglasses, and Katie, the neo-hippie owner of the local skating rink, navigates, her bare feet up on the dash.

A little after seven, we pull into the parking lot of the stadium where the scrimmage is being held, and pile out into the sunshine. Even this early, the heat is visible, the air shimmering over the pavement.

"Ewwww, it's so hot you can smell it." Stella wrinkles her nose.

"Naw, that's your skates," Joe rasps, pinching her own nose in mock disgust. She tosses the keys to Katie. "Your check engine light came on about two miles back."

Katie groans. "Of course it did. I *just* drained my savings to pay to have the AC fixed at the rink."

Joe scrunches up her face in sympathy. "It ain't pipes, so I can't say for sure I can fix it, but if you want, I'll take it over to Pep Boys and pull the codes for you and at least see what's wrong."

Katie flashes her a grateful smile. "Thanks, Joe."

Clapping her on the back, Joe gestures toward the building. "Come on, let's go see what we're up against."

There are several teams warming up already. Joe goes and checks in with the organizers, then comes back to where our team is gathering.

"Okay, listen up. We're going to be skating in the third bout— right after lunch."

Everyone groans at this news, but Joe continues on as if they didn't.

"Stella Be-Red-A will be our jammer. Bexecutioner, pivot. And our blockers will be Lau-Rayna Terror, Katie Kamikaze, and Mandy Mayhem. I want the rest of you to be ready to substitute in. Tina, because of your experience as a trainer, I'm listing you as our second designated staff after myself. Consider your role moral support, but you know, if you want to guide the warm-up?" She pauses to smile at me and I feel an answering thrill—I smile back.

"But don't work them too hard because we still have a while before our bout. Stretch off the stiffness from the drive and we'll warm up on skates later. We'll grab some breakfast at the IHOP down the street, then I want us to watch the first two bouts together as a team. We'll eat a light lunch—save any heavier eating until after our bout."

Joe takes me aside. "I'm sorry if I put you on the spot, but I wanted you to be able to watch from the bench, and if you aren't skating . . ."

"No, this is great. I can definitely help with warm-up and cooldown."

"Okay, good. Here, this is for you." She reaches into her bag and pulls out a Lake Lovelace Rollergirls T-shirt.

"Thanks, that's really sweet." I take the T-shirt, which is vintage soft and purple with white letters. "I'll go change in the ladies' room."

Nipped in at the waist, the T-shirt emphasizes my breasts—it's feminine and pretty. Joe picked a size that doesn't cling and make me self-conscious, but which is still obviously a woman's T-shirt.

The care and thought she put into the gift is touching, and I find myself blushing. I pull my hair into a ponytail and smile at my reflection. Wearing the team shirt makes me feel like part of something larger than myself—an "us," where I've been thinking of the other girls as "them." Somehow my simple thanks seems inadequate, so when I return to the gym, I give Joe a big hug.

"I love the T-shirt. Thank you again."

She holds on to me for a moment, and when she lets go, she's blushing too, and a wave of *wanting* sweeps over me.

"Um, so, I'll go lead the warm-up," I mumble, avoiding her eyes.

"Great, thanks, Tina."

It feels good to be useful, giving pointers on stretches that work the main muscles used in skating.

"And don't forget to stretch your back and your abs." I show them some simple stretches for the core, then help them adjust the stretches to minimize the chances of injury.

"Hey, are you looking for new clients?" Lauren asks. "Because if you can make stretching fun, maybe you could get my big booty moving in the gym." She gives the aforementioned body part a little jiggle.

"I've got cards in my purse. Remind me to give you one later."

"So, are you like a CrossFitter or whatever they're called?" Rebecca asks. I shake my head, ready to talk about how Reed's can certainly accommodate CrossFit workouts, but Stella hoots with laughter.

"Come on Bex, if she were a CrossFitter, we'd all know by now." She pokes Rebecca in the ribs. "Remember how your ex couldn't go a minute without talking about kettle bells and showing off his guns?"

"Truth." Rebecca rolls her eyes. "But I don't think everyone who does CrossFit is as vain as Mike."

"I thought you were gay." Lauren looks between Stella and Rebecca with her brow wrinkled up.

"I'm a unicorn." Rebecca winks at her, and Joe and Stella both laugh.

"Okay, ladies, enough talk about Rebecca's sex life. Let's go get some pancakes." Joe claps her hands and everyone gets up and heads for the vans.

"What did she mean when she said 'unicorn'?" Lauren whispers to me when we're back in the minivan.

"She's bisexual," I whisper back.

"Is it okay to call girls gay?"

"Only if they call themselves gay first. You know Google is your friend, right?"

"Sorry. Are you?"

"Your friend? Sure."

"Gay, goober." She rolls her eyes.

"I prefer the word 'lesbian,' personally."

"Represent." Stella's fist comes between our heads from the backseat, and I give it a bump.

"You guys heard that?" Lauren wails, and we all laugh again.

"Yeah, Lou, we heard. No worries." Rebecca tugs one of Lauren's ringlets. I look over my shoulder and Stella's feet are in Rebecca's lap. Joe and Katie are laughing in the front seat, whether at our impromptu QUILTBAG quiz show or an unrelated joke, I'm not sure, and I don't even care. Everyone's laughing, and I'm a part of something real and fine.

# chapter SEVEN

When we return to the gym, the first bout is getting ready to start. We make for the stands, hoping to get seats where the whole team can sit together to watch and cheer.

"Joe Mama!" A shout from behind us catches Joe's attention, and she swings around, squeals in delight, and runs over to the woman who's called her.

They hug like long-lost lovers; jealousy burns in my stomach.

"You look fantastic, Joanne."

As they pull apart, I study Joe's friend. Tall—she has a type, doesn't she?—with tawny brown skin and sparkling dark eyes. Deep dimples make long grooves to either side of her mouth, and her riot of dreadlocks are pulled into a low ponytail.

Next to me, Stella glares at them.

"What's the story there?" I ask.

"That's Joe's ex," she whispers. "I hate her."

I snort as Stella continues, "It's not enough that she's super pretty, she also happens to be the best skater I've ever seen. And she's *nice* too, so I'm always the asshole for not worshipping the ground she skates on. Bitch."

I laugh out loud that time, but cover my mouth when I realize Stella's not joking. I manage to stifle the laugh before Joe and her ex turn toward us.

"Hey, Red." The woman skates over to us and hugs Stella next. "You look good." Stella gives me a dramatic, horrified glance over her shoulder.

"Paula Fast One, meet Tina. Tina, Paula Fast One."

"Hi." She studies me up and down, not in a mean or sexual way, but definitely taking stock of me. It makes me uncomfortable, but I meet her gaze steadily. Joe's ex. Who she hugged.

"Nice to meet you, Tina." She holds out her hand and I shake it—did I pass some kind of test? "Are you skating today?"

"Tina's a personal trainer. She's helping Joe with the coaching today." Stella throws an arm around my waist. "She'll be skating next time."

"Oh. Fresh meat. Welcome to derby." Paula smiles at me. Even her teeth are perfect.

"Thanks."

She greets some of the other girls and then skates away, locs swinging.

Joe's face is inscrutable as Paula goes.

"So, that was the ex?" I nudge her with an elbow, and she glances up at me.

"Yeah. Chloe—aka Paula Fast One. She's skating in the first bout. I want you and Stella and Bex to watch her carefully—how she breaks through the pack, where she finds her openings. She's one of the best jammers in our league."

Once the bout begins, Paula's dominance on the track is obvious. I hate that Joe's right, that it isn't rose-colored glasses when she looks at her ex—her ex who she's obviously on friendly terms with. Paula Fast One is exactly that—fast, with an eye for strategy, unerringly finding the line through the tangle of skaters.

"See what I mean? I hate her." Stella says after one particularly brutal jam where Paula took a hard hit, wobbled close to out of bounds, but recovered and managed to lap the entire pack.

"Will we have to skate against her?" Lauren asks.

"Not today. Maybe during the regular season." Stella glares down at the track, then smiles sweetly. "Who knows, maybe she'll break a leg."

"Hey." Joe scowls at Stella. "Don't even joke about shit like that. Not even her. She's my ex; that doesn't mean she's evil, okay?"

Stella rolls her eyes and opens her mouth like she's about to argue, but then backs down. "Yes, Wifey."

Stella's acquiescence doesn't lighten the sudden tension between them; if anything, it ramps it up more. She glares at Joe for a long minute, and then shakes her head.

"Why did you call her that?" I ask.

"She's my derby wife. That's like—the person on the team who you meet and you instantly get each other, right from the start. The best friend you've got out there: that's your derby wife."

Chloe's team easily wins their bout. The next bout isn't as dramatic, but Joe brings my attention to different techniques and strategies as it goes on, her voice a low constant in my ear. It's hard to concentrate with her so close—my mouth goes dry and my palms grow sweaty—but I want to please her, want to show her that I'm paying attention, so I force my attention back to the track and watch.

And then it's our turn. As the announcer calls out the name of our team, the skaters pour onto the track and start working the crowd. Then all but the starting five sit on the bench. Joe sits down next to me and leans in to speak.

"The team we're skating against is pretty good, but they've got a few of their best girls down with injury. Their jammer isn't as experienced as Stella."

Stella breaks through the pack first, leading the jam. The other jammer takes off after her, and the race is on. When they reach the pack again, our blockers are ready. Lauren surprises me by landing a brutal hit and knocking their jammer down.

I shout out my surprise, cheering her on, and Joe whistles right alongside me. She glances over, grinning. "And her reign of terror begins."

It strikes me then that Joe has seen this in Lauren all along. She might not be the fastest or the smoothest skater, but she's a fierce and aggressive blocker who isn't afraid to use the full force of her body weight just now in the bout.

During the next jam, their jammer and one of their blockers end up in the penalty box and Stella scores easily against the remaining three on their team.

As the bout goes on, Lauren is replaced by another blocker, and Bex switches places with Stella. Katie comes out a little later, and Lauren goes back in. When a penalty is called on her and she's sent to the box, she grins like it's the greatest moment of her life.

And best of all—we win.

Joe jumps up on the bench and raises her arms. Then she jumps down and hugs me, and we all rush out onto the track to hug our girls.

We watch the final bout, giddy with the thrill of our win, and then we linger, gossiping and chatting with the other teams, but eventually we have to go home. We gather our bags, and we make our way back to the cars. In the hallway, I hear a voice behind me.

"Tina Durham?"

It takes me a minute to place the auburn-haired young woman smiling at me. The last time I saw her, she'd been wearing false eyelashes and a sequin-covered bikini.

"Miss Lake Lovelace."

She laughs with obvious delight. "Amber, please. And I've passed on my crown; I'm not Miss Lake Lovelace anymore. Are you doing this now? Roller derby?"

"Yeah, yeah I am."

"That's amazing. I'm actually working on a story on the resurgence of the sport here in Florida. Maybe you could give me an interview? Former pro wakeboarder finds a second chance with a new sport."

"A story?"

"For the local TV station. Someday, I'm going to be an anchor, but for now I'm working with the sports desk. I've got to run. Here's my card, call me, we can catch up. Congrats on your win today!" She presses a business card into my hand, a kiss to my cheek, and then she disappears.

An interview. I haven't spoken publicly about my retirement or my transition. Ben and I have always laughed at the idea of sports "human interest stories." Isn't it what we do while playing the sport that's really interesting? Then again, I never saw the appeal of a press conference either, and I did plenty of those. But it would be nice to catch up with Amber. I tuck the card into my pocket and rush to catch up with the rest of the team.

"I'm so freaking beat, can someone else drive?" Joe is asking as I approach the van.

"I've got it." Katie takes the key. "It's my van anyway."

"Shotgun!" Lauren calls, and everyone stares at her. "What, I have kids. We do that."

We all laugh.

"Joe, you and T sit in the back; you can stretch out and get a nap." Stella takes one of the captain's chairs in the middle, and Bex takes the other. I squeeze between them to get into the backseat, and Joe joins me.

"So, your first bout. What did you think?"

"It was amazing. I could see your whole strategy play out—who you put where and why. My God, Joe, it was . . ." I shake my head. "It was the coolest thing I've ever seen. And I was there when Ridley Romeo landed a nine hundred in the double-up contest, so that's saying something."

She laughs and stretches. "I'm glad." Then she shivers. "The AC is super cold back here."

"There's a blanket." Bex calls. "It's behind the seat."

Joe finds it and scoots closer to me. "We can share."

She wraps the blanket around us. Cocooned in the backseat, we talk about the bout, comparing notes on what we saw, until she falls asleep with her head in my lap.

My heart pounds in my ears. My hands clench at my sides—where do I put them? I slide one to the soft curve of her waist, above the blanket. After the van hits a big bump, she startles a bit, but settles down when I smooth her hair away from her forehead. It's exquisite, beautiful agony, the hour I spend with her sleeping in my arms.

When she finally wakes, she blinks up at me and smiles, then touches the side of my face. She pushes herself to a sitting position, lays her head on my shoulder, and we ride the rest of the way home like lovers.

That night, we meet up at Blue's for celebrating and drinking. The beer is delicious and cold, and the company friendly and warm. When someone starts dumping quarters into the old jukebox, tables get shoved aside and the dancing begins.

Dancing always makes me feel self-conscious, but I love watching the others. Lauren is a fantastic dancer, hamming it up as she moves, laughing and swaying with easy grace.

Joe grabs her around the waist and pulls her into an embrace, and a flash of jealousy works through me when they both laugh. It's ridiculous, of course. Lauren is married, and I straight-up told Joe I wasn't looking to get involved. I did that, and I don't get to take it back.

So why am I frowning into my beer at the sight of my two friends sharing a hug?

"Tina, you should dance, come on." Stella grabs my hand and starts towing me toward the makeshift dance floor.

"No, I'm too . . ."

"Too what? Anxious? Shy? Oh, honey, nobody here is judging you. We don't care whether you got all the moves." She squeezes my hand. "We won our bout! We're celebrating. Celebrate!"

I take a final swig of my beer and set it on a table, then follow Stella's lead onto the floor. She puts her arms above her head and swings her hips with a sensual fluidity I can only imitate, but I do, gamely, and I grin like I mean it.

"Like this." Joe's voice rasps behind me, and, like always, it sends a shock of craving through my body. Her hands settle onto my hips, and she spins me to face her.

"Hey." She smiles at me, wide and guileless and lovely.

"Hi."

"Bend your knees a little, scoot closer." She hooks her fingers through my belt loops and tugs me close until my leg is between hers and our hips are grinding together. "Yeah. Put your hands on my waist."

Her tank top is damp with sweat, and I fight the urge to push the soft cotton up and away so I can run my hands over sleek skin.

She releases my belt loops and drapes her arms over my shoulders, leaning back to smirk up at me.

"Just like that." Biting her lip, she closes her eyes, and I lose myself in the sensuality of dancing with her, of the warmth from her body and the rhythm of our hips pressing closer and then swaying away.

She's everything, in that moment. The rest of the world ceases to exist. I want to hold on and never, ever let go.

"What are you doing to me?" I murmur, and her eyes pop open in surprise.

"Nothing you aren't doing to me," she whispers. "Come home with me, Tina. No one has to know."

I peek around the room, but nobody pays attention to us, and the music covers our whispers.

"The team." I try one last time.

"I think they've got enough to gossip about with those two, don't you?" She gestures with her chin and I glance around. Stella is making out with Rebecca in the hallway leading to the bathroom, their bodies pressed close, her hand on Rebecca's ass. They're sexy as hell together, and I can't help the little sound that escapes me.

"You knew about them before today?"

"I suspected. Stella's always had a thing for goth girls, and Rebecca . . ." She shakes her head. "Rebecca is hard to resist."

"Are you speaking from experience?"

"Nah. Not with Rebecca. But look at her."

I can see her point. Rebecca is one of those girls who exude confidence and a certain naughty sex-kitten appeal. The Bexecutioner is a favorite with our derby crowd, winning them over with equal parts sass and skill.

"Yeah, I get it. Confidence is sexy." I duck my head, faltering in my rhythm.

"Hey. You know what else is sexy?" Her hand cups my face, draws my gaze down to hers.

I shake my head.

"Being vulnerable and trusting. The way you look at me sometimes . . . shit, Tina. You should come with a warning label."

My cheeks flush hot at the praise. "You know what I really want?" I whisper, changing the subject to safer territory.

"What?"

"I want to skate. I watched you guys today, and that was awesome, but it made me hungry."

"Well. That's a hunger I can do something about."

"Yeah?"

"Yeah. I have the keys to the rink. It's closed, but Katie won't care if I take you there after hours. You can get it all out of your system. Come on, I'll drive."

We say our good-byes to the rest of the team, and I follow her out to her van. She grabs my hand, threading our fingers together, and grins at me.

"Skating. I never quite know what to make of you."

I look down at our joined hands, a smile spreading across my face. "You do okay."

The drive is short—only a few minutes later, we're unlocking the back door of the rink, Joe's skates dangling from their laces in one of her hands, the other clutching mine.

"You can use rental skates." She nods toward the shelves with their neat rows of sturdy brown skates with orange wheels.

I grab a pair and lace them up, struggling with the short laces on the right boot.

"Hold on a sec," Joe says. "I'm gonna see if I can get the sound system going."

She disappears, and then the lights come up over the rink and the speakers throb to life. Some ten-year-old Rob Thomas song starts pounding through them, and Joe's laugh fills the empty rink.

"Sorry, I can't do anything about the music selection. I don't think Katie's been able to afford to update for a while."

I shrug, stepping out onto the smooth floor and sliding over to her. "I like pop music."

"So, what do you want to do? See how fast you can go? Practice jumping?"

I turn around so I'm skating backward, and grab her hands. "Like dancing, but . . ."

"Hmmm. I like that." She takes the lead, and I fall into step, letting her turn us and guide me around in a big, lazy circle. "It's good for your footwork too. You're a really talented technical skater."

"Thank you."

"I should test you again at the next practice."

"Yeah?"

She nods. "I think you'll pass."

"No one will cry favoritism? After I left the party with you?"

"Oh, they might." She spins me around so fast I almost fall, and the thrill of it makes me giddy and giggly. "But they'll see you skate, and they'll know you earned it."

"I work hard."

"I know you do. And sometimes, I think you're better at this coaching stuff than I am."

"It's my job." But then I think of Jeremy and his shaking legs, and think maybe I have a ways to go there too. "But let's not talk about that. Let's just skate."

I drop her hand and swing around so we're facing the same direction, and I pick up my pace. She laughs and follows *my* lead, and the race is on.

She's fast and fearless, and by the time the songs have changed twice, we're both sweating and laughing, and that achy, wanting feeling in my chest has finally disappeared.

"I needed this," I mumble breathlessly.

"We should go. It's getting late."

"Okay, I'll meet you over by the rental skates. I really gotta pee."

In the restroom, I splash cold water on my face. What the hell am I doing? Joe is the coach. And no matter how friendly she seemed with Chloe, there was obviously some painful history from the way Stella acted. I don't need to be getting in the middle of any drama.

But this is Joe. Exuberant, sweet, sexy Joe. And God help me, I want her.

"Tina? Where are you?" Joe's voice is full of laughter as she rounds the corner and spots me struggling with my laces. "Are you stuck?" She doubles over with another round of giggles.

It's contagious, apparently.

"Shut up." I laugh in spite of myself. I can't help it: the music, the skating, the rush of being here, in the dark, after hours. Permission or not, it feels like we're getting away with something, which speaks to that dark little part of my soul that always wanted to rebel, even when I still thought fitting in was the greatest victory. "There's a knot in my laces. Stupid rental skates."

"Here, let me." She kneels at my feet. "I'm good with knots."

She pulls my skate onto her knees and starts working on it, her face side-lit by the neon over the concession stand. There's a softness, an innocence even, to the curve of her cheek that stings my heart. How many people get to see this side of Joe Mama? Suddenly I'm very conscious of the fact that my foot is in her lap, and my breath catches. Her gaze flickers up to mine, her silver-and-black lined eyes sparkling.

"Got it," she whispers. Pulling the laces from the eyelets, she slides her hand up the back of my leg; a burning trail of awareness follows her palm along my skin to where it rests behind my knee.

The side of her mouth twitches up in that half smile, the one she must have practiced in a mirror. How else could she have nailed that casual sexiness so perfectly? Her other palm cups my heel, and with a quick tug, the skate slips free.

The smile falls away, but she doesn't break my gaze.

My foot in her lap. Her hand behind my knee. A dawning appreciation crackles between us in a continuous circuit.

Her eyes close, and she makes a sound low in her throat—a pained, lusty noise like sex and deprivation together. Leaning forward, she kisses the inside of my knee. The press of her lips is dry and warm, and gone too soon, as she turns her head to the side and lays it on my lap, trusting as a kitten with her affection.

"Tina," she whispers.

My hand settles onto her hair, my chest is heaving like I've run for miles, and the silly, giddy rush of a moment ago has given way to a body-tightening arousal.

"Joe, we need to—"

"Shhh." She sits up and touches a finger to my lips, her eyes wide and solemn in the semidarkness.

All the reasons not to get involved—holy shit, what would the team say?—spark around us like electricity in the air before a storm, but I don't care. I catch that finger with my teeth.

We both go still and silent, frozen. Did I go too far? My heart gallops in my chest, exultant and terrified at once.

The next moment, she's in my lap, straddling one of my legs, and I've got an armful of sweet, sexy Joe as she presses her lips to mine.

The kiss is raw and hungry. One of her hands tilts my face up; the other tangles in my hair, not tugging, but holding me close. She moans and her hips roll against me.

I run my hands up her back. I clutch helplessly against strong muscles, slide my tongue into her mouth, and ride the wave of lust surging between us.

"God," she gasps, moving her lips from my mouth to my jaw, then my neck, then a quick nip at my ear.

Shivering, I scratch slowly down her back, my nails catching slightly in her ribbed tank top. She arches and I lay my head against her chest and catch my breath to the sound of her heartbeat thudding in my ears.

She tilts my chin up again and smiles. "I'm so wet right now."

Her words send a jolt through me, and I groan, desperate to feel her, to taste her. I settle for biting at her nipple through her shirt and sports bra. She yelps, then her sounds turn urgent and needy. I cup her other breast in one hand, teasing the nipple with thumb and forefinger, learning which touches makes her cry out and rub herself against my leg. She's fearless in sexual abandon, her mouth falling open and her hands pressing me closer to her breast.

"Goddamn," I murmur, tugging at the hem of her shirt so I can finally, finally get at her skin.

"Yeah." She yanks first her shirt, then her bra over her head. I barely have time to drink in the sight of her full breasts and tight brown nipples before she reaches for my clothes.

A wave of tension — not the good kind—hits me and I grab her hands and push them behind her back, making her arch and sigh.

"Let me see you too," she whispers, her voice ragged with need. "I'm so fucking turned on."

"In a minute." I kiss her again, holding her hands behind her back and teasing her until she softens against me in acquiescence. I'm not sure where the sudden nerves came from, but the way she lets me take over until I get them under control gives me the confidence I need to let go of her hands and reach for the buttons on my shirt.

"Let me." She gently pushes my fingers away and slips the button free. "Don't you think undressing a lover for the first time is like unwrapping a present?"

*A lover.* The word sends a thrill through me, and tears sting my eyes. I drop my hands and she works down the front of my blouse, kissing the skin she exposes with each button she frees.

"Oooh, look at you," she croons, and the admiration in her voice makes me squirm toward her. She slides her fingers over the turquoise lace of my bra. "I shoulda known you'd go for the pretty, girly stuff. It's so sexy on you." She pinches one of my nipples through the rough lace, sending a jolt from breast to groin. Like my body is one big tuning fork, vibrating to some note made just for her. The rasp of lace against skin is hot, but I want more. I want her mouth on me. I want wetness and heat and oh, God . . .

She unhooks the clasp of my bra and draws it down over my arms. It lands silently on the pile of clothes accumulating behind her.

Her hands find my nipples, tweaking and pinching, and each touch ignites me. A shiver works down my spine, and my hips rock up to rub against her. I'll never get enough of the taste of her skin or the way she feels in my hands. I trace my fingertips from the inky blue tattoos on her shoulder across her collarbone and down to tease her nipples the same way she's teasing mine, and she arches back, laughing.

How long has it been since I laughed with someone during sex? Have I ever? It feels good, shameless and free. She bites the side of my breast, her breath wet and hot there, then trailing slowly across to my nipple.

My whole body tightens in anticipation as her lips close over my waiting flesh.

I shiver, caught in the rush of heat. My limbs go lax as she draws on my nipple, again and again. One hand slides down to cup me through my pants, and instead of pushing it away, I ride her hand as another kind of pressure builds inside me.

"Yeah, rub off on me," she whispers, "Can you come like that?"

I don't know, but it would take an act of Congress to keep me from trying.

She moves her hand in gentle circles, and my hips take up the rhythm. I want her hands on me, not my jeans, but I'm too far gone to tell her; instead I'm biting the heel of my palm to keep from shouting as I come, eyes clenched shut, my whole body shuddering under the swell of pleasure.

"That's so fucking hot." She watches me with lust-filled eyes as I catch my breath. She picks up my hand and kisses the heel of my palm right over my teeth marks, wrenching another shiver from me.

I don't even hesitate. "Come home with me—please?"

We stare at each other in the dark—if she comes home with me, that means something. It means more than a furtive grope.

"I'd love to."

We pull up in front of my house and she lets the van idle, watching me as I fidget in my seat. "Are you having second thoughts?"

"I—" I gesture to my house "—I bought this place with Lisa." And for some reason I can't really articulate now, it makes me feel bad and ashamed, and so completely unsexy.

"And you don't want to bring a new lover into your old marriage bed." Joe nods. "I get it."

That isn't exactly it, but it is part of it. "It's more that . . . it's full of reminders of all the ways I don't feel good enough to be with someone."

"I think there's two paths this can take." She reaches across the console and takes my hand, lacing our fingers together. "Because I think you're wonderful. I think you're thoughtful, and funny, and fearless, and totally sexy. And I want you to feel good, and I *don't* want to do anything that makes you feel bad. You with me so far?"

"Yeah."

She smiles then, and brings the back of my hand up to her lips. "Okay, so option one: I go home. We had fun, but you aren't ready to take it further, and that's okay."

I start to protest, but she squeezes my hand and I shut up and let her finish.

"Option two: I wait here in the car while you go inside and pack an overnight bag. You get Elvis, and as much food as he needs for the weekend, and the two of you come to my house. I make you come at least one more time tonight, and then you cook me breakfast in the morning."

A little laugh bubbles out of me. "I cook you breakfast?"

"Yup. I have a waffle iron." She raises an eyebrow. "Just saying."

"And do I get to make you come too?"

"If you like." Her grin spreads across her face. "My place is a no-bad-feelings zone. Nothing but orgasms and waffles, I promise."

How can I say no to that?

A half hour later, I'm following her through the door to *her* house, butterflies in my stomach and Elvis at the end of his leash beside me.

She flicks on the light, stoops, and unclips Elvis's leash from his collar so he can explore. Then she straightens and takes my hand, pushing the door shut behind us with her foot.

"Do you want a tour?"

I shake my head, mouth dry.

"Good," she whispers.

She backs me against the door and rises on tiptoe to fit herself along the length of my body. In the past, my height compared to cis girls has made me uncomfortable, but she just presses into me and covers me with herself until there's no room for awkwardness. The kiss is gentle, an envoy, an exploration—barely more than an exchange of breath, but somehow heavy with expectation.

God, I love kissing her.

I peel up her tank top, and she breaks the kiss and lets me tug it over her head and toss it aside. *Beautiful.* I run a hand from the whorls of tattoos on her shoulder across the satin-smooth skin of her clavicles, feeling an answering excitement in myself when goose bumps break out under my fingertips.

"Take me to bed?" I mumble against the side of her neck, tasting the salt of her skin there.

She backs away from me and leads me down the hallway to the bedroom. She moves through the dark as I stand in the doorway, and turns on a small lamp next to the bed. I get an impression of softness: an artfully peeling antique dresser and creamy drapes, a mountain of gold cushions piled on the bed. It's *pretty*—somehow elegant and comfortable together, the kind of space to invite late nights and lazy mornings.

Crossing the room, I tumble her down onto that mountain of softness and taste her mouth again, this time letting the urgency rise slowly in me. This time we have the rest of the night to enjoy each other, and the anticipation is a potent turn-on. She tugs off my shirt, and I stand up to kick off my jeans. I pull her cargoes down her legs to find bright yellow boy-style briefs with black piping underneath. So absolutely, perfectly her—as playful as they are sexy.

Propping herself on her elbows, she smiles and cups the side of my face with one hand. Her thumb travels across my cheekbone, then down to my lips. I turn my face into her palm, close my eyes, and let her hold me like that for a minute, tears stinging my eyelids, because this tenderness from her, this sweetness *hurts*.

"Teeeeee-na." That voice. That broken little singsong makes me blink back the tears and look up along her body. "Take off my underwear." She gestures toward them with her chin.

I shake my head, and instead kiss her through them, letting my breath touch her first, then my tongue through damp cotton. Her head drops as I inhale the musky-sweet scent of her.

"Tease." She chuckles as she says it, and I ease her briefs to the side so I can slide my fingers through slick heat and rub a thumb across her clit.

"Oh, fuck *yeah*." She's practically molten in my hands as I lean forward and taste her. *Sweet.* I trace circles over her swelling clit and stroke inside her with two fingers. The way Joe—gorgeous, take-charge, fix-everything Joe—goes slack and loose-limbed in pleasure sends a wave of heat through me. And then, as she gets closer to orgasm and her movements pick up again, there's so much trust, so much openness in how she lets her body thrash and writhe.

"Oh fuck, fuck, don't stop." She buries a hand in my hair and holds me where she needs me. I stiffen my tongue against the sensitive underside of her clit and she comes completely, beautifully unglued, her shoulders lifting off the bed and her whole body racked with a deep shudder. I stay with her through it, my fingers working inside her as I lighten the pressure against her clit and gently bring her down from her peak.

"Oh my God," she murmurs. "Holy fuck, get up here and kiss me."

Laughing, I tug her yellow briefs back into place, giving her one last stroke, and then kiss my way up her body. She seizes my face with both hands as she kisses me, hard and deep. Then she rolls me over and nibbles and licks from my breasts down my stomach, pausing to blow into my belly button and make me laugh. My laughter turns to a delighted shiver when she bites the inside of my thigh, but I stiffen up as she reaches for my panties.

"Is this okay?" She strokes my side. "Do you want me to slow down?"

I shake my head. "No. But you're the first since my divorce. I feel . . . God, I hate talking about this."

"You don't have to say any more. I understand—maybe not totally, but enough. Do you believe me when I tell you you're sexy?"

Does wanting something badly make it true? I want to believe her, and maybe it's that easy.

"Yes. I believe you."

"I'm really enjoying myself—" she traces a hand down my thigh "—and I want to make you feel good." She nips at the hollow of my belly. "You're sexy, and I'm into you."

And then she gives my panties a tug, sliding them off my legs and tossing them over her shoulder. She takes her time—running her hands over my thighs, kissing the insides of my knees, and lavishing my hip bones with gentle bites until the tension slips out of my body and I sink back against the bed. Then, when my eyes drop closed, she finally touches my clit. I'm so turned on, both from the way she's touching me and from the excitement of going down on her, my body practically hums with it. The first touch of her tongue is soft and slippery, and her fingers gentle as she slides them into me.

She looks up. "Touch your breasts; show me what you like."

I cup my hands over them, plucking my nipples and pinching them nearly to the point of pain as she watches, still rubbing gently inside me.

Her thumb rolls over my clit, and the first tremor of orgasm hits me, a hint of what's in store.

"Please," I whisper, pinching my nipples again. She rubs faster and heat washes over me. I can't keep my hips still; they roll up into her, and I'm riding her hand when she leans closer and sucks my clit gently. The tightness coiling in me releases and I arch up, shaking.

"So fucking sexy, Tina." She says it right against my clit, the vibration of her voice sending another shudder through me. Then her tongue is on me and I let go with a wild shout.

Afterward, she pulls the blankets around us and spoons me from behind. "That was really fun," she says. "I'm glad we decided to have a sleepover here, because I want you for second breakfast tomorrow."

On Sunday morning, we cuddle up on Joe's couch with coffee and our phones, the smell of waffles lingering sweet and heavy in the air. It's an easy laziness, with nowhere to be and nothing to do but enjoy her company. Her feet are in my lap, her toenails an appealing glittery teal, and her body shakes with laughter at something on the screen of her phone.

"Stella changed her relationship status on Facebook to 'in a relationship' but Bex's says 'it's complicated.'"

"Oh boy."

"Yeah. Gonna be some dramarama at practice next week."

"They make such a cute couple though."

"Uh-huh." She twists around and sits up, moving to straddle my lap. "So, I want to meet your friends."

I flinch. Not because I don't want her to meet Ben and Eddie—that particular introduction is inevitable—but because being with Joe feels too new, and I don't want to share her yet.

"Soon," I whisper, pulling her into a soft, coffee-flavored kiss. "I'll tell them to come to a bout once I make the team."

"Oh, then I'm definitely doing assessments this week." She pulls away from me, laughing. "I want to meet this Ben dude."

"Ha! That's the perfect word for him. Ben is *such* a dude."

"But he's gay, right?"

I nod. "Yeah, and he's engaged to a cute younger guy. At first, they don't make sense, until they laugh together, and you see the intense way Davis looks at him, like the whole world could be unraveling around them, and nothing else would matter but Ben."

"Whoa." Joe raises an eyebrow.

"Yeah." I don't tell her how I understand what Dave must feel in those moments now, because it's got to be like what I feel when Joe touches me. It seems too soon, too big, and all of a sudden that ache in my chest is back.

"Was that weird, when you guys were riding pro? I mean, extreme sports don't seem to be the most queer-friendly."

What? Oh, Ben.

"Um, not really? He wasn't exactly out on the circuit. Of course, there were rumors. He wasn't closeted, and people made jokes about him and Eddie all the time, but he would just shrug 'em off. Said to deny it would insult Eddie, so he'd rather ignore it. And after his accident, it was moot. People don't give a fuck about you once you stop competing."

"So, forgive me if I'm prying, but I'm fascinated by these gay guys you grew up with. They knew you were trans?"

"Before anyone else did." And *I'm* suddenly fascinated by the ice-blue glaze on her delicate little coffee cups. I trace it with my finger. "Before my family. Before my wife."

"Wow."

"Yeah. Lisa has plenty of reasons to be mad at me, but the one I regret the most was hiding my dysphoria and eventually the beginnings of my transition from her as long as I did. Ben knew when we were teenagers. And even though Lisa and I were high school sweethearts, I didn't come out to her until the night before the press conference where I announced my retirement. I started hormones about six months later."

"Holy shit, Tina, the night before?"

I swallow around the big lump in my throat. "Yeah. I'm an asshole."

"No, you're not." She shakes her head and pulls me down into a snuggle. "You're human. And I'm selfish enough to think maybe things didn't work out with Lisa because the universe meant for you to come into my life when you did."

"I was a mess when I was with Lisa. And I'm not just talking about before my transition. I let her take care of everything, take care of me—and I kept this huge secret from her because I was scared to be alone. And the longer I live by myself, the more convinced I am that my fear was only partly about losing her, and more about having to take care of myself."

"You guys were practically kids when you got married though. Don't you think some of that is natural?"

God, she's so sweet. "It's really nice of you to try to make me feel better about that; I'm not sure I deserve it though. I broke her trust long before she broke my heart."

"Why did you stay together so long after you transitioned if there was so much broken stuff there?"

"We loved each other. I was still crazy about her, and she loved me too. For a while, when everything was changing so fast between hormones and then surgery, she focused on supporting and taking care of me—she was always good at that. We thought there would be some imaginary finish line, after which our marriage would be something different. During that time, the promise of a finish line was enough. And then everything *was* different, and we were in a relationship she never imagined for herself, and it wasn't enough anymore. So, she asked me for a divorce."

"I'm sorry."

"I understand how relationships are supposed to work. I get that everyone makes sacrifices and compromises for love. But the things we needed—" I don't realize I'm about to cry until the little sob catches my voice. I wipe at my eyes and shrug. "We both needed things we couldn't give each other."

"I think you're amazing."

And I don't know what to do with that. I'm not amazing. Because if anyone is amazing, it's the girl who built a derby team from scratch with nothing but enthusiasm. Not me.

But before I can say anything, a thud sounds from down the hall, and Elvis's toenails skitter wildly on the hardwood floors toward us.

"What the fuck?" The words spill out of me.

We both sit up just in time to see my dog careening wild-eyed into her living room, tangled up in something, with a—*a dildo?*—thumping along beside him.

"Oh. My. God." Joe shrieks with laughter and rushes to help him, repeating a seemingly endless litany of "Oh-my-God oh-my-God oh-my-God." As soon as Elvis is free, she holds it up. "He somehow got under the bed and twisted himself up in my strap-on."

The howl of mirth that comes out of me shocks Elvis and sends him scurrying under the couch.

"Oh, no, buddy, I'm sorry, come here. I'm not laughing at you or that big mean penis that was trying to get you, I promise."

I can barely breathe as I say it, unable to stop giggling even with my dog shaking and glaring at me from under the sofa.

"Ohmygod. Big mean penis. Ohmygod, you just said that." Joe doubles over, a high whine of hysteria escaping her.

I somehow manage to collect myself enough to coax Elvis out, and the three of us collapse on the floor.

"What do you do with that thing, anyway?" I ask between bursts of giggles.

"Um . . . you're kidding?"

I shake my head, wide-eyed. "I mean, I know what it's for, but it seems like . . . if you wanted to have sex with a penis-having person . . ."

"Okay, stop right there. Just because I'm a lesbian doesn't mean I don't enjoy penetration or doing the penetrating." Her voice drops to a sexy purr. "I happen to love getting a woman all hot and bothered and begging for my dick."

Her words burn through me like wildfire, as arousing as a physical touch, and I squirm.

"You call it that? Your dick?"

"When I'm talking dirty, sure." Her pretty bow-shaped mouth turns up in a smile. "We can try it sometime if you like."

Wow. The world seems a lot bigger and a lot smaller than a few minutes earlier—bigger because there's this possibility I never imagined, and smaller because there doesn't seem to be enough air in the room for me to answer her.

"Think about it," she murmurs, brushing a kiss over my cheekbone. "No pressure, but if that's something you want to do, I think it would be super hot."

"I think it would be too." I don't know where the words came from, but I can't deny how much the idea excites me.

"Yeah? What turns you on about it? How do you picture something like that? I'd like to do it sitting down, with you on my lap. I could play with your clit and your nipples while you ride my dick." She bites her lip and her eyelids droop a little, but she's watching me intently.

"Hearing you talk like that turns me on. I don't know why. I never . . . I've always liked women. Maybe it's because mine was a source of dysphoria for me, but penises don't turn me on, and dildos remind me of dilating. I've never really thought about being on the receiving end of—" I gesture toward the strap-on and blush. "So I don't know why it turns me on. Do I have to know?"

She smiles and shakes her head. "No, of course not. Knowing that it does is good enough for me. I like knowing what turns you on, gets you hot. I like talking about it and thinking about it." She sets the strap-on aside and slides her fingertips along my thigh. "I especially like how talking about it makes you blush and squirm."

She pulls me into a kiss, and my eyes slip closed. Elvis scrambles away from me, to where I have no idea, and the next thing I know, Joe and I are stretched out on the floor and her tongue is in my mouth. The carpet abrades our elbows, our shoulders. I don't care. She shoves away my pants, pushes up my T-shirt, and bites the hollow of my belly, the edge of my ribs, the bottom swell of my breast. My skin aches and swells everywhere she touches me, and I want to bottle this raw honesty, this naked need that lets me guide her down my body until her hands and tongue shake me free again.

# chapter EIGHT

"**S**omebody had a good weekend."

"Excuse me?" Is Nate actually leering?

"Durham, you got a love bite the size of Texas on the side of your neck."

My face flushes hot and I rip my ponytail holder out of my hair as he chuckles. At five in the morning, depleted from a weekend of derby and sex, I forgot the souvenir Joe left on my skin.

"So, who's the lucky—guy? Girl?"

"Girl." I confirm. "I can't tell anyone—it's a secret."

"Durham, you're too old to have a secret girlfriend. Grown-ass women shouldn't hide their girlfriends in the closet."

"Butt out, Nate. It's more complicated than that; nobody's in the closet, and you're my boss, not my dad." I make my way to the ladies' locker room and check out my neck in the mirror. With my hair down, the hickey is hidden, so I leave it like that. Maybe I can run home on my lunch break and cover it with concealer. When I return to the weight room, Jeremy is there, slurping the last of his protein shake.

"—I'm telling you, you never seen anything like it, these guys were piling out of the dugout and onto the field. It was *insane.* Oh, hey, Tina." He turns to me. Nate gives us a little wave and goes back to his office.

"Hi, Jeremy. How's everything going?"

"Okay, I guess. I had some dizzy spells over the weekend, like I'm getting a sinus infection in my ears or something, so we should take it easy today."

"Are you eating?" I try to keep my voice neutral.

"I told you that was a stupid mistake!"

Nothing neutral about his voice.

"I'm just asking."

"Yes, I eat."

"Okay. Did you run here today?"

"No, I drove 'cause it's raining and I'm out of Body Glide."

"Okay, do a nice, slow mile on the treadmill to warm up and meet me back here by the weights."

He doesn't make it to the treadmill.

His knees start wobbling as he walks away, and then he crumples, right in front of me, like a wind dancer when the air turns off.

"Jeremy!" I'm at his side in an instant, rolling him to his back and checking for contusions. "Nate!"

"Jesus, what happened?" Nate rushes over, pulling out his phone. "Elevate his legs. Is he breathing? Check his airway.

"Yeah, I need an ambulance sent to nine-nine-seven-two Alligator Avenue. I've got an unconscious man in my gym . . . a moment ago. No. I don't know. I have no idea—twentysomething. No, no drugs, the kid's a health freak. Well, I don't know. No. Not in my gym."

Jeremy's chest is rising and falling, and I can feel air moving as he breathes, so I pick up his wrists to take his pulse. Holy shit, it's fast.

"His pulse is racing."

His hand jerks in mine, then he blinks at me. "Where am I?"

Relief knocks me over. Slumping against a rack of weights, I close my eyes and try to calm my own rapid heartbeat. "Reed's Gym. You fainted."

"No way." His voice goes thin and wavering. "Like in the movies?"

A hysterical giggle slips out of me. "Yeah, like that. You even just asked where you were. Has this ever happened before?"

"I feel really dizzy." He starts to sit up, but I still him with a hand on his shoulder.

"Stay put, your heartbeat is super fast. Nate's called an ambulance."

"An ambulance? Dude, no. I just need to take it easier."

"Jeremy, you haven't even started your workout. This isn't a matter of going at it too hard. You fainted on your way to the treadmill to warm up."

"My heart feels like a fish flopping around on the dock." He puts a hand over it and winces.

"Um, yeah. You're *definitely* going to the hospital."

"Ride with him, Durham. I'll cancel the rest of your clients today." Nate is still hovering with his phone to his ear.

"Tina?" Jeremy's voice is tiny and scared.

"Yeah?"

"Will you call my mom? And Emily?"

"Of course, hon. Where's your phone?"

"In my locker."

By the time I get off the phone with Jeremy's mom, the ambulance has come and gone. Contrary to what you see on TV, I don't ride with him. I've told his mother I'll meet her at the hospital, so I call the girlfriend on my way.

When I get there, a whip-thin redhead in butterfly scrubs behind the ER intake desk blanches visibly and shakes her head. "I'm sorry, it's family only."

"I just got off the phone with his mom; she knows I'm coming. He's expecting me."

"I'm sorry, sir, I can't—"

I reel back like she's slapped me. My jaw drops open and I force it closed. I haven't been misgendered in months. What the fucking *hell*? Fear washes over me, a quick wave of it, followed by anger, shame, and a rush of nausea.

"I'm a woman," I whisper, and she has the decency to blush.

Carefully pitching my voice exactly as I was taught to sound as feminine as possible, I speak slowly. "I'm his personal trainer. I was with him when he collapsed. His doctors will want to know what's going on. Please let me talk to them."

"There you are." A tall blonde woman comes out from a hallway to my left. "I thought you'd gotten lost. You're Tina, right?"

"Ma'am, it's family only." Butterfly Scrubs stands up at her desk.

"I'm his mother. He wants her here; I want her here. She was with him when it happened."

My nausea is replaced by gratitude.

A young woman in a sundress bursts through the doors and runs over to Jeremy's mom. "Karen, where is he? Is he okay?"

The two women hug before turning to me.

"Emily, this is Jeremy's trainer." Karen introduces us with a gentle smile.

"You're the one who thought he had an eating disorder?" Emily takes my hand between both of hers. "He doesn't, I swear." And then she bursts into tears.

"We're going back now." Karen glares at Butterfly Scrubs and leads us all down the hallway, filling us in as we walk, stopping in a small waiting area immediately inside the Russell Cardiology wing.

"They're doing an electrocardiogram to look for irregularities in the electrical signals in his heart. Something about an arrhythmia causing the rapid heartbeat. His pulse rate has started to return to normal, so they might not find anything, but they might."

"I'm sorry I accused him of having an eating disorder," I say softly.

"He's eating fine—cooking from scratch too." Emily's smile quirks up on one side. "He really felt bad about what happened that morning. He respects you so much, and he hated that he disappointed you."

A lump forms in my throat. My impossible, impulsive client is lying in a hospital bed with wires and electrodes measuring the electrical signals in his heart, and his girlfriend is talking about the bright side of me mistaking it for an eating disorder?

"Why are you both being so nice to me?"

"Because outside of his family and very close friends, you're one of the people he trusts the most." Karen pulls me into a hug. "And because you were with my baby when he was scared, and that made him less scared."

"I don't know what to say." I snuffle into her shoulder, and it hits me then—he may be difficult, he may be stubborn and secretive and a royal pain in the ass to train, but Jeremy is my *favorite* client. So I say that, because it explains everything. "He's my favorite."

Karen squeezes me tighter, then lets go, but before she has a chance to say anything, a nurse in plain pink scrubs comes over and takes Karen aside. They speak in hushed tones for a few minutes, and then the nurse walks away.

"Well, the ECG is done. They're going to have the doctor read it and come speak to Jeremy. Tina, he's asked for you."

He doesn't look sick, lying back against the pillows in the propped-up bed, jiggling his foot impatiently.

"Hey, you." I sit next to him. "I guess you're skipping leg day. Slacker."

He laughs. "Is my mom pissed?"

"Your mom cares that much about leg day?"

"Nah. Is she pissed I asked to speak to you first?"

I shrug. "Doesn't seem like it. I like her."

"The doctor said I might have a heart condition—I'm waiting to hear from the MRI how bad."

The words are like ice water to my face. Is he sick? Dying?

"What does that mean?"

"For starters, I'm probably not going to be able to do the bodybuilding competition." His face falls, but then one of his eyebrows arches. "But he said other than that, I'm in awesome shape."

"Of course you are."

"So, I'm gonna miss my sessions for a while, and I think the hospital bill is going to be pretty insane."

Ah. Yeah. Financial stuff. "I'll get your automatic payments put on hold until you can resume your workouts again."

"Thank you. I know you're missing work and stuff. You don't have to sit with me, but I'm really thankful you came."

I stay with him a few minutes longer anyway, but when the doctor comes in, followed by Jeremy's mother and girlfriend, I say my good-byes and get out of there.

I call Nate, but he's already canceled my training sessions, so he tells me to take the rest of the day off. Alone with Elvis in my empty house, I send a text to Joe.

*Having the strangest day. Miss you. Can't wait to see you at practice.*

Maybe a half hour later, she texts back.

*Strange how? I miss you too. My day is a literal shit show.*

*My favorite client fainted. I went to the hospital. Now it's 10 a.m. and I'm off for the rest of the day.*

*Is he okay? She?*

*Maybe—they're running tests. Anyway, sorry your day is "shitty." ;)*

*Ah, the glamorous life of a plumber. Are you going to call the beauty queen from the TV station?*

I've forgotten all about running into Amber at the scrimmage. I pull out her card and stare at it. The idea of talking about my former career fills me with sick dread.

*I don't know. How is there any way it doesn't turn into a story about me being trans?*

*Would that be a bad thing?*

*It's scary. I don't want people to make a big deal out of me.*

*You are a big deal. And when it comes to sports stories, you're the real deal. I think you should do it. But I'm selfish. I wanna see your face on TV. See you tonight. xo*

I have a lot on my mind between Jeremy and the reminder of Amber's interview request, and on top of that, I'm antsy from missing my morning sessions. I always do my best thinking while exercising, but it's too hot to take a long walk with Elvis, so I call Ben and ask if I can use his swimming pool.

"Sure. Dave's there, working on wedding stuff, so, you know, knock before entering, et cetera."

Dave lets me into the house, brings me a bottle of water, and tells me to let him know if I need anything. Elvis, who wants nothing to do with the swimming pool, stays in the shade while I swim.

Physical activity has always been a form of meditation for me, swimming especially. There's something about the feeling of weightlessness that melts worry from the body. Why am I afraid to let Amber interview me? I'm not ashamed of who I am, or who I was. I don't like attention, and I don't seek it. But is it more than that?

I float on my back and stare up at the bright blue sky, moving my arms just enough to keep myself afloat. An interview would be good press for the Lake Lovelace Rollergirls. But at what cost? Would they get transphobic assholes showing up at the bouts? None of us need that.

Eventually, my fingers turn to prunes, and my limbs start to get tired. I have to get out of the water, so I wrap myself in a fluffy towel and head inside.

"Hey. I'm making lunch; I was about to bring you a sandwich." Dave smiles at me and places the sandwiches on the breakfast bar. "So what's going on? Why aren't you working today?"

I explain the situation with Jeremy, the canceled clients, and then my dilemma regarding Amber's interview proposal.

"Can I ask you something?" His gaze pins me with its quiet, serious focus. "When you were fourteen or fifteen, if you had seen an interview with someone like you—a trans adult, happy in her career and personal life, how would you have felt?"

The question is a punch to the gut. Because I know—*I know* it would have meant everything to me. It would have answered questions I didn't know I had. It would have been solidarity in a time of turbulent solitude.

Before I can say anything, he continues, "There are trans kids out there—and trans adults, for that matter—with parents like my stepdad."

As if *I* don't know that? "I know. And I think Amber would get it right."

"Don't do it for your team or for Amber. Do it for the kid you were. She needed this, and she didn't get to have it. But other trans kids can. You can be that person for them."

"I'm a personal trainer, not a superstar. I'm not a role model. I'm just me."

"But that's my point. Kids don't need superstar role models. They need to see people they can relate to."

I don't even realize I'm crying until Dave wraps his arms around me. I cling to him, getting his shirt all messy, and it's awful and embarrassing, but I can't seem to stop.

The glass door slides open. Ben walks in and finds us like that, and he snuggles up to the other side of me, takes a bite out of my sandwich, and pats my shoulder until I get the tears under control.

"Are you guys doing some kind of silent communication thing?" I mumble, snatching my sandwich back.

"Nah, I knew you were going to be here, and him, so I took a boat from the dealership and came home for lunch."

"I cried on your fiancé."

"He'll be all right. He has at least six blue polo shirts just like that one. So, what's with the waterworks?"

"I'm going to do an interview with the local TV station about derby. And about wakeboarding."

Ben lets out a low whistle. "On television?"

I nod. "Yeah."

"Well, good for you. Does Eddie know? We could do an ad buy for the shop during your segment."

I smack his arm. "I'm getting emo over here, and you're plotting your advertising budget. Cold."

"I love you, Tina. You're going to be great, because you're always great. You're funny, you're smart, you don't have to work hard not to say 'ain't' like a big ol' redneck. Damn right I want an ad for my pro shop to run in the middle of your perfection."

I can't help it; I laugh, and let them hug me again. Ben swipes the rest of my sandwich, Dave makes new ones, and by the time I leave their house, I've got an appointment the last week in August with Amber at the television station to tape the interview.

# chapter NINE

**t**hat night at practice, with heavy-duty makeup covering the hickey on my neck, I wait nervously with the other fresh meat as Joe and Stella set up cones at regular intervals down the length of the gym.

"Suicide sprints are a simple concept. You sprint to the line, then you sprint back to the wall. Then you sprint to the next line, then back to the wall. But we're putting a little derby twist on it. At each line, you execute a safe fall. Remember to tuck up, fall small. Then get your ass up and get back on the wall. One rule: you can't do the same fall twice. Go."

I'm sweating after the first fall, when I drop to my knees. By the second, my legs are aching. By the third, I'm mentally cussing out Joe and Stella, who watch us from the sidelines.

I was a professional athlete. *For years.* And I'm struggling.

When I collapse on the floor at the end of the drill, every part of my body hurts. Joe skates over to me.

"How's it going?"

"The *M\*A\*S\*H* theme song is a lie." I groan. "Suicides aren't painless."

Joe laughs and sticks her hand out, hauling me back to my feet. "You did great."

And then she skates away. No hug. No flirting. None of the easy affection I've gotten used to from her.

My stomach lurches and I blink back the sting behind my nose. *What the hell?* Did I imagine our intimate weekend together? I know we can't let on to the rest of the team that we're seeing each other, but she's treating me like a stranger. And it hurts.

As the rest of the skaters finish, Joe and Stella set up the cones in a different configuration—four cones to mark the inside corners of a track. Joe skates to the center of the room and dangles her stopwatch in the air. "Since you're warmed up, who's ready to do 27/5?"

A few of the other new girls gasp. Doing assessments *after* suicides?

Some of the assessments I've already passed. Safe falls I can do. Lateral jumping, I'm all over that. Speed isn't a problem usually—but I've never had a speed test after suicides. I don't need anyone questioning whether I can hack it. I don't need to be questioning it myself.

When the whistle blows a few minutes later, I push as hard as I can, and then I push harder. My lungs are burning, my legs protesting. My heart pounds like a heavy-metal drummer in my chest. And I push on. Heading into the last straightaway, I swing my arms and give it everything I've got. I fly past Joe, who calls out my time.

"4:38. Nice work, T."

Slowing to a stop, I brace my hands on my knees and gulp in air in huge, heaving breaths. I still need to jump the sack at the end of the obstacle course. In order to make the team, I need to jump the sack. I can do it. I know I can—I've mastered lateral jumps, and managed a few head-on jumps in the last couple of practices, but it isn't the same as jumping under pressure.

I stare at the sacks of sand, just sitting there, taunting me.

"You can do this." Lauren skates up to me. "If I can do it, *me*? You can totally do this."

"I think I need to be alone for a minute."

I skate out into the hallway and sink down against the wall. I pick at the end of my purple LLRG laces, which I lovingly moved from the rentals to the new Riedell skates I bought when I decided yeah, I really wanted to play derby. All I need to do is jump the sack. I've learned how to take a fall, so even if I trip—or fudge the landing—I'm not likely to get hurt. The only thing stopping me from doing this is my stupid anxiety.

"Tina?" Stella comes out to the hallway. "You okay?"

"It's just a sack of sand."

She grimaces. "It's your bugbear. Lauren's was the 27/5. Yours is jumping."

"Yeah."

"So, look, you're a damn fine skater. You've got more natural talent and balance in your little toe than a lot of us have in our whole bodies. You could be every bit as good as Paula Fast One or Joe Mama, or any of the badass derby babes we all love. You just gotta get your head in it."

"I know."

"Joe isn't gonna wait for you, honey. You need to go back in there and jump that fucking bag before she moves on to the next drill."

"Okay."

She reaches out a hand to help me up, and I take it.

Back inside the gym, my hands shake, and I draw in as many deep calming breaths as I can manage.

"Tina, you're up." Joe says. "One successful run through the obstacle course, and you're a Lake Lovelace Rollergirl."

One successful run after twenty-seven laps and suicide sprints. Easier said than done.

The obstacle course changes slightly every time. The cones are set up in a line, and I need to weave in and out of them like a sine wave. Several members of the team are standing alongside the course in their sports bras, with their stinky, sweaty shirts balled up in their hands, ready to throw at me.

And at the end of it all is my bugbear. The sack of goddamn sand.

A woman who made a career out of jumping on water should not be afraid of jumping over one little sandbag.

Joe blows the whistle. I throw myself forward, straight toward the cones. The first T-shirt comes flying at my face, and I duck. The second is aimed at my feet; I weave. A shirt soars straight toward the middle of my body—but too slow. I let it hit my flank, stink and all, and fall to the floor behind me. I clear the last cone and speed toward the sack.

Every ounce of my focus narrows to that harmless-looking gray sack.

"Butt down, Tina!"

I get low. I bend my knees. I take a deep breath—and I *fly*.

It's inelegant, and my landing is awkward and scary and involves a tiny bit of flailing. But I'm upright. I cleared the sack.

I've made the team.

And I start crying for the third time that day.

Three of us make the team that night. Over beers at Blue's, Courtney becomes Wynona Spider; Jennifer becomes Jenny from the Glock; and when asked, I say the first thing that pops into my head: "Hoochie Glide"—my favorite wakeboarding trick.

"You know we're all gonna shorten that to Hooch, right?" Stella cackles, handing me another beer.

"Hooch it is." I grin. "Where's Bex?"

She rolls her eyes. "Went back to work after practice. She's got appointments booked until ten every night this week."

"Oh."

"Yeah. But I'll see her later." She gives a coy little smile and pushes at her afro.

"Hoochie, can I speak to you?" Joe comes up behind me. "Somewhere private?"

Stella glances between the two of us. "We're talking, Joe."

I take a sip of my beer and study Stella's face. She looks—not mad, but *hurt.*

And honestly, I'm hurt too. Joe's been ignoring me all night, and I don't much feel like talking privately, but I push that down and swing around to face her.

"Yeah, *Coach.* Where do you want to go?"

She flinches at the word "coach" and then gestures with her head toward the parking lot. "Come sit in my van. It's quiet out there."

Stella has folded her arms over her chest and is biting her lip like she's trying to keep from saying something.

"Red?" I ask. "Do you mind?"

"You don't need my permission to *talk* to Joe." She's speaking to me, but she's looking at Joe when she says it, and something about the way she emphasizes the word "talk" feels like a warning. Does she know about us?

I follow Joe out to the parking lot, anger blooming in me with every step. The heat in the air seems to intensify my frustration—if we weren't keeping secrets, we could be having this conversation in the comfort of air conditioning over cold beers. Although, if we weren't keeping secrets, we wouldn't need to have this conversation at all. By the time we get to her van, I'm so pissed I'm shaking. As she starts unlocking the door, it bursts out of me.

"If this is how you treat all your lovers, it's no surprise Chloe left you."

She rears back and her face hardens.

"Get in the van. We're not doing this out here."

"Why not? My day has been shitty enough. Why not make a big old spectacle of myself over a girl? I mean, we're supposed to be celebrating, right? I made the team, yay!"

"Stop it." She pushes her fingertips into her temples. "Stop and think about what's happening here."

"What's happening is that you're ruining *everything*." I start toward my car, too pissed and hurt to stay and talk it out.

"Tina, please." It's the catch in her voice that stops me. Her small, broken voice with its sexy rasp, trying to make something bigger of itself to call me back, and it crumbles there, in the middle of the word "please."

"Don't yell. It's not worth the risk." I turn back to her. "I'm not worth the risk."

"You are. Will you please come talk to me?"

I can't resist her when she says "please." I get in the van, and she immediately starts the engine and turns on the air conditioning. It feels like heaven.

"I'm so sorry, Tina. I didn't mean to let you think I was ignoring you or mad at you. I might have overdone it a little in trying not to show any favoritism."

"You made us do *suicide sprints* before the assessments."

"And you passed. No one can say you didn't earn that. No one."

"What does it even matter if you're going to treat me like a stranger in front of the team? If you keep that shit up, everyone's going to know we had sex anyway. They'll just think one or the other of us was terrible at it."

"I'm sorry. I was nervous too, okay? I was nervous about your assessment. I was nervous I made it too hard. I was scared you weren't going to pass. And I kind of shut down because I couldn't let any of that show."

"But what are we *doing*, Joe?" Nate's words from the morning come back to me. "Aren't we too old for secret girlfriends?"

"I don't want it to be a secret forever. I just—can we just keep it quiet until I figure out how to tell the team? Please?"

She picks up my hand and nibbles at the tips of my fingers, sending a sharp pang of lust through me as I remember all the ways she used her teeth on me over the course of the weekend.

"I won't pretend we're strangers." She bites the inside of my wrist, and my head drops back. "Come back to my place for orgasms and waffles. Please?"

Her voice breaks again on the "please."

"I think you do that on purpose." I sigh, pulling her toward me. "And I am so weak for it."

Her lips meet mine in one of those kisses that stings the heart. She can hurt me—she already has, and could again. The kiss is my protest, and her apology, and all the pain between them.

But when she bites my lower lip and then tongues the sting away, it takes the other hurts with it, and forgiveness tastes a little like blood and tears.

# chapter TEN

he alarm on my phone goes off at 4:30 a.m., like always, but it takes me a moment to remember that my five thirty client won't be meeting me at the gym. I turn it off and roll to my side. Joe's arm wraps around my waist and pulls me back into the curl of her body.

"Do you have to go?"

"Not yet."

"Good."

We doze a little longer, and around six, my phone rings. Jeremy. I slip out of Joe's bed, leave her with Elvis curled up at her feet, and take the call in her kitchen.

"Jeremy, how are you?"

"Already jonesing for my missed leg day. I thought you'd want to know what's going on. I mean, since you were there yesterday when it happened."

"Of course. Are you feeling okay?"

"Still having the dizzy spells, and they have me on a heart rate monitor. I have a heart condition called Wolff-Parkinson-White. Turns out I was born with it."

"Is it . . . is it treatable?"

"Yeah, they do a thing where they stick catheters in my leg and zap parts of my heart until it's normal again."

"That's it?"

"Well, the procedure isn't painless or anything, so there's a recovery time. But yeah, basically, that's it. We're doing the procedure tomorrow, and then I can resume normal workouts in about two weeks—earlier if I feel up to it."

The relief that swamps me then—I didn't realize until that moment just how much guilt I'd been carrying over his illness, whether it was an eating disorder and I'd missed the signs, or had been working him too hard in the gym. Not only is it neither, but it's also treatable, and he'll be back to normal in a matter of weeks.

"God, Jeremy. That's . . . I'm so fucking relieved."

"I knew you'd understand. I was so worried I was doing something wrong. And I skipped breakfast that morning and—"

"No, honey, that was my fault. I jumped to conclusions—"

"But that's the thing. We were both wrong. I was wrong about being a fuckup, and you were wrong about being a fuckup too. We're okay, right?"

I can't hold back a laugh at that. "Yeah, we're okay. I expect you back at the gym, unless I hear otherwise, at 5:30 a.m. two weeks from Monday."

Thankfully he drops the phone before cheering. Then he picks it up again. "I'm the biggest asshole in the cardiology wing. I should go; Emily is giving me the look."

"Feel better soon, Jeremy."

"I will. Hey, did you mean what you said to my mom?"

"Which part?"

"That I'm your fav-or-ite."

Good grief. This kid. "Yeah. I meant it."

"You're my favorite too. Bye, Coach!"

And he hangs up like it's nothing.

"*You* are all mine tonight." Stella grabs me as I come through the door at practice, steering me away from where the fresh meat are doing blocking drills. "I didn't get a chance to see you again after you and Joe disappeared last night, and of course she didn't tell you my plans for you."

"I'm sorry—we were in the van, and she was my ride home, and Elvis hadn't eaten—" I'm babbling excuses, but she brushes them off.

"Come on, we're going to play a little game called 'pass the panty.'"

"Okaaaaay." I glance around, looking for Joe, and spot her explaining something to one of the newest recruits, a skinny blonde with eyes like saucers. She smiles when she sees me and gives me a little wave. Relieved, I wave back.

"Earth to Hoochie." Stella snaps her fingers in front of my eyes. "Okay, so Joe and I talked about it, and we want you skating pivot. You're fast *and* big, so who better to put in a position where you could be either a blocker or a jammer? So, what we need to do is practice pulling the panty off our helmets and passing it hand to hand while skating. Lauren, Bex, and Katie are going to be trying to fuck up our pass and force a penalty on us. Lauren's husband, Chase, is joining us tonight to play zebra. He'll call it if we make a bad pass."

Sure enough, there's a guy standing with Lauren and Bex. He's a hefty guy with ruddy round cheeks and dark curly hair shot through with gray. So that's Chase. He laughs at something his wife says, and then looks down at the stack of papers in his hands.

The drill is intense—the blockers go after us aggressively, and it takes several tries before Stella and I manage to complete a panty pass without dropping it or being forced out of bounds.

I'm starting to hate the sound of Chase's whistle.

And then there's getting the panty over my helmet without taking a hit.

"This is why we have to practice it." Stella gives me a hand up from the floor. "You're doing great, by the way."

I flush at the praise, because it sure doesn't feel like I'm doing great. I hand her the panty back. "Hold on, I gotta get a drink of water before we go again."

I skate over to my bag and dig out my water bottle, taking a long drink. Joe skates over. "You okay?"

I nod. "Yeah, but this drill is so hard."

"It really is; that's why it's so important. How's it working out with Chase? I talked to him about maybe learning to ref, so he and the kids can be involved and he won't feel left behind."

"That was a good idea. Lauren said she hoped he and the kids would come to some bouts." I take one last pull from my water bottle before tossing it back in my bag. "It adds to the realism of the drill, too."

"Tina!" Stella shouts, and I glance up. "This isn't social hour."

Joe flinches as though the scolding was meant for her. "Okay, I gotta get the fresh meat working on some speed drills. I'll come check on you and Stella in a minute." She reaches out and gives my hand a quick, furtive squeeze, and then she's gone.

"You guys coming over to Blue's?" Stella asks as Joe and I skate around, picking up the cones. The others have gone, and it's only the three of us left.

"Nah, not tonight. I'm beat." Joe's gaze flickers up to meet mine.

"Me too. Maybe next time." I give a little stretch. Shit, is that too obvious?

"All right." Stella pauses and stares at us for a minute. "I guess I'll go over to Bex's shop and hang out while she sketches. Maybe if she has a cancellation, I'll get a tattoo." She turns to leave, giving us one last look over her shoulder.

"Have fun! Good work tonight," Joe calls after her.

"Okay." Stella waves and then the door swings shut behind her.

"Oh, finally." Joe drops the cone she's holding, skates over to me, and wraps her arms around my waist from behind. I relax into her embrace. "I've wanted to touch you all night."

"Me too," I murmur. "Well, touch you, I mean. I touch myself whenever I want."

Her laugh vibrates through both of us. "Hmmm, maybe later you can do that while I watch. Bet it's sexy."

My exhaustion fades and my heart rate speeds up. I turn around and lower my lips to hers, bending my knees a little to bring us closer to the same height. She takes the hint, slides her hands up to my neck, and opens for me.

I don't know that I'll ever get enough of the noises she makes when we kiss. I yank her tank top up so I can splay my hands out against her skin, feel her warmth and her sweat, the way she shivers from head to toe at the contact.

"Hey, did you guys see my—" Lauren's voice startles us apart. We spin away from each other and stare, horrified, at the door.

Lauren stares back, her face turning red. "I'm sorry. I didn't know—I mean. I need to find my phone."

She practically runs up the stadium seats, taking them two at a time and looking both ways. "Found it! Okay, I'm gonna—I'm gonna go."

"Lauren, if you could maybe keep what you saw between us, that would be—" Joe glances at me, apology in her eyes. "I haven't figured out how to tell the team yet."

"Okay. Good night." Lauren doesn't meet either of our gazes as she books it out of the gymnasium.

The door swings shut again, and I let out my breath in a great *whoosh*.

"Well."

"Shit." Joe sinks to the floor and sits. "I'm so sorry."

I sit next to her and pick up her hand. "What are you sorry for? It takes two, you know?"

"I should have known better. People come back for stuff they forgot all the time. And we got caught by *Lauren*. The straightest straight girl on the team. I don't think she can even say the word 'lesbian' without blushing. I mean, at least if it were Stella or Bex . . ."

Remembering Stella's response to seeing Chloe at the scrimmage, I shake my head. "I don't think it would have been a good thing if Stella had caught us."

"Stella's cool, she wouldn't say anything to anyone."

"She probably wouldn't say anything, but I don't think she'd be too cool about you sleeping with someone on the team."

Joe drops her head and then meets my gaze. "You don't think—"

"Did you *hear* the way she talked about Chloe?"

"You have to understand, those two—"

"No. Whatever that was, it was about you."

She frowns, then scrubs a hand over her face. "Okay, yeah. There's some history."

"Want to fill me in?"

She sighs. "Not really, but I guess I should. We all three used to skate together. I was a blocker, the two of them were both jammers, so they had a friendly rivalry thing going on. Before Chloe and I broke up, we were fighting all the time, and I left the team because it wasn't any fun anymore. Stella blamed Chloe."

"She blamed her for you leaving?"

"Yeah. You know all those little rivalry jokes she makes? They weren't funny anymore because since then she's sounded like she meant them."

There had definitely been an edge to Stella's commentary the day I met Chloe. "Go on."

"I started the Lake Lovelace Rollergirls six months later because I missed derby like crazy. Stella, because she's my friend, went from being on the best team in the league to being the only veteran skater on a new, unseeded team that can't even field fourteen skaters."

"Oh." But that seems all the more reason to keep us a secret from Stella. Wouldn't she be afraid of something like that happening again? What does this mean for me and Joe? Before I can ask, Joe continues cheerily.

"Anyway, Chloe and I fixed our friendship after our breakup, but Stella never forgave her—or maybe she never liked her to begin with, and didn't have to pretend anymore now that Chloe isn't dating her best friend."

"And you don't think she'd be mad at me for dating you?"

"Of course not. What reason does she have to hate on you?" She lets go of my hand and stands, her voice and expression falsely bright as she says, "Come on, nothing to be done about it now. Let's finish up here and get home. Will you come over? Elvis is welcome, of course."

"You are in total denial, but yeah. I'll come over."

Joe's shoulders slump and she lets out a broken little noise—not exactly a sigh or a sob, but something in between. "She holds me to a higher standard than maybe she should. I'll figure it out."

Then she holds open the door to the gym, making it clear that conversation about Stella is over.

At home, a steaming-hot shower washes away my sweat and sore muscles. I linger in my closet, trying to decide what to wear, and finally settle on a short-sleeved shirtdress. Comfortable, cute, and—most importantly—easily removed.

I gather Elvis and his food and drive over to her place, worrying the whole time about how Stella would react to Joe getting involved with me. But wouldn't anger be hypocritical since she's sleeping with Bex? I've gotten to like Stella and trust her, and it would hurt to lose her friendship.

However, all thoughts of Stella disappear when Joe answers the door in a pair of striped boxer briefs and one of those white tank tops of hers with no bra underneath. I unclip Elvis and toss his leash aside, unable to take my eyes off her.

"Wow. Goddamn, you look sexy in men's underwear."

She laughs and throws her arms around my neck. "I love that you like me in men's underwear, because that lacy, girly stuff you wear would drive me crazy. It suits you though."

"Mm-hmmm. Too bad I didn't wear any tonight." I push the door shut behind me and let her press me up against it. "Where were we, back at the gym?" I slide my hands up under her shirt, tickling the still shower-damp skin there.

"Ooh, we were definitely getting there." She unbuttons the top button of my dress. "I love buttons. I love opening each one—" then the second "—and seeing each tiny little bit of your skin appear."

She presses her lips to my clavicle, and my eyes drift closed. The next button slips free and she buries her face between my breasts. "I love the way you smell. I get wet when I think about biting you here." She sucks a red bite to the inside of my breast. "So wet."

"I want you to fuck me," I blurt out, and she draws back.

"Are you asking for me to strap on my dick, Tina?" Her lips curl up in a sexy smile. "Want to feel me deep inside you? Want to ride me?"

Oh God, hearing her talk like that in her raspy voice makes me feel hot all over. "Yeah. God, your voice is pure sex."

"You want to eat my pussy? I want that. I want you to lick me until I come on your face, then take my dick like a good girl."

I could come just from listening to her talk. The things she's saying, yeah, they're filthy hot, but it's the crude, bossy way she says them that makes me moan.

"Or maybe I'll finger you first, but I won't let you come. Maybe I'll keep you right on the edge until you ask me nicely."

She cups me low, the heel of her palm pressing into my clit and her fingers teasing my entrance. Looking into my eyes, she smiles that dirty smile of hers, and I shudder all over.

"Do whatever you like to me." I gasp. "But don't stop talking."

She bites the side of my breast again and shoves the dress off my shoulders and down my body. A button skitters across the floor, and holy shit, she's actually ripped my clothes off. I shove the heel of my hand into my mouth to keep from crying out.

"You're a tiny bit kinky for the dirty talk, aren't you?" She brings her hand from my pussy up to her mouth and licks it in one long, slow, deliberate movement. "Mmm. Come on, let's go to bed."

She leads me, naked and stunned, to her bedroom and shoves me down on the mattress. Not gently, but I don't need gentle. It's not like I'm going to break. I need *her*.

She reaches into the drawer beside her bed, but she doesn't pull out the strap-on. Instead, she grabs a blue vibrator and a bottle of lube and sets them next to me on the bed. She strips off the tank top and boxer briefs and crawls up my body, sliding one of her legs between mine and bracing herself there.

"Kiss me." It's half command, half plea, and I'm powerless to resist either. Her tongue slides into my mouth to feint and fight with mine. My breasts press against hers, and I rock my hips so her thigh rides along my sex.

"Mmm, that's good." She picks up the vibrator and holds it to my lips. "Suck my dick; get it nice and wet."

I take the blue silicone into my mouth. It feels weird, and not sexy, but I'm still riding her leg and she's looking at me like she's *proud* of me, and I want her to keep doing that. So I moan around it, getting it sloppy with spit. She pulls it away and then sits back and studies me.

"Spread your legs."

A hot flush washes up my chest as I do what she asked. She turns on the vibrator and presses it to my clit.

I nearly shoot off the bed, the rush of sensations shocks me so much.

"Ooh, my girl likes that," she croons, sliding the vibrator around my clit until I moan and relax against the pillows. My hips won't stop moving. Her other hand comes up and squeezes a breast, teasing at my nipple. My brain doesn't seem to be able to choose which to focus on: the intensity of the vibe or the pinch on my nipples.

"Good girl," she rasps, then takes my hand and moves it to the vibrator. "Hold this while you lick me."

Her words make me shiver as she positions herself over my face, and I remember what she said downstairs. *Lick me until I come on your face, then take my dick like a good girl.*

I almost come. It's too intense, so I abandon the vibrator to spread her open with both hands and run my tongue along the underside of her clit.

"Fuck, yes." Her hand slides into my hair—a caress and a demand. "Don't stop. Such a good girl." Her voice gets raspier and I cling to her thighs, holding her still against my lips. "Tina, God, *Tina.*"

She shudders with the force of her orgasm, and repeats my name over and over. As her body quiets, I loosen my grasp on her legs and ease her down for a kiss.

Clearly unfazed by the taste of herself on my mouth, she wraps her arms around me, laughing. When she catches her breath, she whispers. "Ready for my dick now?"

I can't speak, so I nod, and she kisses me again, a quick press of her lips to mine.

Closing my eyes, I bite my lip as she touches the vibrator back to my clit. *God.* And then she opens the lube bottle and starts talking and I nearly lose it.

"Good girl. I'm going to wet up my dick for you. Get it nice and slippery. You want me to fuck you?" The vibration disappears for a moment, but then she slides the slick vibe into me, and I about come unglued when it hits the perfect spot. Oh God, am I coming? My shoulders fall back against the bed, my hips lift, and the orgasm seems to well up from some deep place inside me. There's so much pressure that when it releases, I can't stop shuddering, and she angles the vibe so it hits that spot again. I cry, I beg, I babble, and I ride that amazing orgasm to the depleted end.

All while she tells me I'm her good girl.

When I'm nothing but a warm puddle of satisfied bliss, she turns off the vibrator, pulls it out of me, and stretches beside me, covering my face with kisses. "Oh my God, that was . . . I've never talked so much dirty in my life, but the way you kept getting more and more turned on, that was incredible."

"You're so filthy. I love it." I don't know if I can move my legs, but I *love* it.

"I hope you don't mind that I didn't get the strap-on out."

"Is that what started this? I don't care if we never play with the strap-on. As long as you never stop talking dirty."

"I promise." She kisses me, long and hard and deep, and then tucks me into bed.

After turning off the lights, she joins me under the covers. I fall asleep with my arms around her waist, my head pillowed on her breasts, and her voice teasing my ears. Cherished.

I can't think of anything more perfect.

# chapter ELEVEN

"tina, thank you so much for coming." Amber greets me at the local television station with a smile and a hug. In a simple blue suit, pearl earrings, and low heels, she is unrecognizable as the bedazzled beauty queen I met a year earlier.

"You look great, Amber."

"Thank you. So do you. If you'll follow me, I'll take you back to makeup."

It occurs to me, as we make our way through the maze of hallways, that she seems a little young to have landed a job at the station.

"If you don't mind my asking, how are you working at the TV station if you're still in college?"

"It's an internship. I mostly research sports stories and help write them, but my mentor here at the station is allowing me to do a special-interest segment once a month. Since you represent old-school Lake Lovelace wakeboard royalty *and* the hot new sport in town, you make a super fascinating story."

"So who's going to be interviewing me?" Panic sends my blood racing.

"Oh, that's me. I'll be on set with you, and Scott—my mentor—will be producing the segment. We'll have three cameras on set—one on me, one on you, and one pulled back to get both of us at the same time."

Forty-five minutes later, both of us are wearing heavy TV makeup and sitting in oversize chairs under a bank of hot lights. The producer, a balding, beak-nosed man with hipster glasses and a graying goatee, comes over to introduce himself before the interview begins.

"Ms. Durham, it's a pleasure to meet you. I'm Scott Sorenson."

I barely manage to croak out a "Hello" over my sudden onset of anxiety, but he just smiles.

"I know this is nerve-racking. But the segment will be prerecorded and packaged, so don't worry too much. This isn't like a press conference, where we'd be asking tough questions or trying to get a scoop. This is a feel-good story."

Whatever that was supposed to mean. If it's a feel-good story, shouldn't *I* feel better about it?

"*Weekend Sports* airs in the evenings, so Amber is going to say 'Good evening' when she opens the interview. I know it's morning now, but just roll with it. We're going to cut in with footage of you wakeboarding, as well as footage of you playing derby. We'll be recording your practices this week, and we'll likely interview some of your teammates and friends as well. So I'm clear—you do prefer female pronouns, is that correct?"

"Yes."

"And when we speak about your past career, prior to transition, which pronouns would you prefer we use?"

"My pronouns are still female pronouns. I was assigned male at birth, but I am *not* male, and I have never *been* male. Thank you for asking, by the way."

He nods, then continues, "When we talk about your wakeboarding career, we'll do what we can to refer to you only by your last name. Should we need to use a first name, we'll only use your dead name if it's absolutely unavoidable."

"I appreciate that."

"Thanks again for being here." He smiles and returns to his position behind the cameras.

It's go time.

"Good evening, and welcome to *Weekend Sports*. I'm Amber Wilson. My guest tonight is a two-time winner of the Lake Lovelace Wakeboarding Tournament—but postretirement, her athletic career has taken an exciting turn. Welcome, Tina Durham, aka 'Hoochie Glide' of the Lake Lovelace Rollergirls, to the show."

The butterflies in my stomach give one last lurch, then I smile. "Thank you, Amber, I'm happy to be here."

Saturday morning on Labor Day weekend, I wake up to the bed shaking. I roll over and Joe is curled onto her side, coughing into her fist.

"That doesn't sound good."

"Stupid summer cold." She flops back onto the bed. "I had the smallest tickle in my throat yesterday, and now I feel like death warmed over."

Poor thing. Her eyes are glassy and her face red—from fever? Or from the exertion of coughing? Oh God, her voice.

"Is coughing going to do something bad to your vocal cords?"

She shakes her head. "Nah. I might lose my voice, but it should come back. It's really unlikely that any further paralysis will happen."

"You're flushed." I put my hand on her forehead—it's hot to the touch. "I think you have a fever. Stay put, I'll get you some Motrin."

"Thanks. It's in the medicine cabinet over the sink. Left-hand side."

I get up and head to the kitchen, start a pot of coffee, and pour a tall glass of water from the pitcher in her fridge. On my way back down the hallway to the bathroom, I fetch the bottle of Motrin and bring them both to her.

"You're a lifesaver, thank you." Sitting up, Joe takes the water and drains half the glass before opening the medicine bottle and swallowing down two pills with the rest of the water. I sit down next to her and take her hand.

"I'm making coffee. Do you want any?"

She shakes her head. "I hurt all over. I'm going to try to sleep some more."

"I'm supposed to go hang out with Eddie and his boyfriend today to watch the double-up contest. I'll call and cancel."

"No, don't. I'm just going to sleep all day. Go be with your friends."

Elvis jumps up on the bed and noses his way between our joined hands. We both laugh, but then Joe's laugh turns into a cough, so I grab her empty glass and take it back to the kitchen for a refill. When I get back, she's stopped coughing, and Elvis is curled up against her side.

"You have *totally* stolen my dog." I hand her the glass.

"Can he stay with me while you're off watching your contest thing? I've got the chills and he's so warm and snuggly."

"Of course. Are you sure you don't want me to cancel? I don't mind reading a book or watching TV while you sleep."

"No. You go. We'll be okay, won't we, Elvis?" She kisses the top of his head, and he snorts happily and wags his tail.

Inside, I'm relieved. I've been looking forward to spending time with Eddie. I've barely seen him since I started playing derby. But I feel like a lousy girlfriend—even a lousy secret girlfriend—for not staying and taking care of her. She told me to go, right?

I put some food in Elvis's bowl and leave it on the kitchen floor, then fill his water bowl and set it down beside the food, then return to the bedroom.

"Okay, I put food and water out for Elvis. If you want to let him out in the backyard, I'll clean it up when I get back later. Call me or text me if you need anything, okay?"

"Thanks, T." She reaches up for a hug and I kiss her briefly on the lips.

"Feel better, baby."

Elvis, the big traitor, doesn't even look up when I leave.

Traffic near the marina is insane, and I had to run by my house for my swimsuit, so I'm late getting to the slip where Eddie's cruiser is docked. When I finally sprint up the dock toward it, he's standing on the deck, pulling out his phone.

"Sorry I'm late. Is everyone here already?"

"It's about time." Eddie rolls his eyes dramatically. "And yes, everyone is here except you and Elvis. Where's the mutt?"

"He's with Joe." I untie the first line and toss it to him. "She has a summer cold, and I left him with her to cheer her up."

"And who, Tina-cakes, is Joe?"

I undo the second line as he pulls the bumpers inside the boat. I use the rope in my hand to pull the boat close enough to the dock, and then hop across, taking Eddie's waiting hand to steady myself.

"Joe is a new friend. And she is way cuter than Ben." I find myself grinning at our old joke. *A friend like Ben? Or like a* girl*friend?*

Eddie finishes packing away bumpers and ropes, so I start stripping down to my bikini. For as long as I've known him, Eddie's boats have been places of sanctuary for me, places I can be free and comfortable in my own skin, my own name, my own pronouns. So when he shouts, it startles me.

"What the hell happened to you?"

I glance down at my leg—green and purple bruising runs from my knee to my hip. I touch it and a goofy smile spreads across my face. "Nasty fall. Not a serious one though."

"It sure as hell looks serious." Oh, that's rich, coming from Eddie. The guy goes out to sex clubs and comes home bashed up like he's been in a fistfight. "And what are you grinning about?"

How to explain it? That the way I feel about derby is like falling in love? "You know how when you meet someone, and you get all wrapped up in them, giddy at the thought of them, and the time you spend with them seems brighter and more intense than anything else in your life?"

He peeks up then, not at me, but at his hot younger boyfriend, who's slapping sunscreen on his shoulders and grinning at a gorgeous lady who must be his mom. Wow. Good genes. Eddie's face gets soft and sweet, an expression I've never seen on it before. Holy shit. Eddie Russell is completely smitten.

"Yeah, I know what you mean," he says, still making heart eyes at his lover. Then he looks back at me, a little flushed and unfocused. "So, you feel that way about this Joe?"

*Yes.* The intensity of the thought takes me by surprise. I laugh, and I lie. "Nope, I feel that way about *derby*."

"Derby? Like, roller derby?"

"Yep." I tickle his ribs. "You should come see our next bout."

His face changes and he goes into business mode. "I can do that. Send me the details, and Wish and I will make a date of it."

I have no doubt that they will. Eddie takes his social calendar seriously. It's one of the things I like best about him—his ferocious commitment to his friends. But there's something else there too—the way he's including Wish, drawing him into our circle. That's almost as big a hint about the nature of their relationship as that sappy eye-fuck he bestowed on Wish.

"I saw you look at him just then," I tease.

"So what?" He turns a glare on me, and I laugh, holding up my hands.

"Nothing, not saying a word. Put some sunscreen on my back, okay?"

# chapter TWELVE

On the night the interview airs, Stella's boss closes the bar for a private screening for the team. My hands shake and knees wobble as I explain to them that the interview is me publicly coming out as trans after years of quiet retirement, but the girls all hug me and tell me they're excited to see it. That goes a long way toward calming my nerves.

Stella brings me a beer in the back corner booth. I have a decent view of the massive wide-screen dominating the space over the bar, but I'm separated enough from the rest of the team that I don't feel like I'm under a microscope.

"I'm so proud of you." Joe, sitting across from me, squeezes my hand.

The theme music for *Weekend Sports* starts, and before I'm even prepared for it, Amber is introducing me.

"Oh God." I scrub both hands over my face. "This is really happening."

"Oooh, your hair looks so good!"

I manage a wan smile at Bex.

Amber's first question gets right to the heart of things. "Tina, you're the first transgender athlete we've had visit us on *Weekend Sports*. Is there anything off limits for tonight's interview?"

The me on the screen smiles nervously. There in the bar, I mouth along with the words. "My ex-wife, my current relationship status, and the contents of my underwear."

Under the table, Joe's foot bumps mine, and I look up to see her staring at me, wide-eyed. "Thank you," she mouths. I shrug. It hurts me, the fact that she still hasn't told anyone about us yet. I understand why—and I don't begrudge her the time to figure out how best to tell the team—but a part of me wants her to stand up and say, "Hey, I'm hers, she's mine, and if anyone has a problem with it, tough."

On the screen, a home video plays of teenage Ben and preteen me sitting on the sundeck of Eddie's daddy's MasterCraft and talking about the air we were gonna get that summer. Ben looks like a young blond god, all muscle and smiles. I look like a kid. The camera pans right to show two alligators sitting on the bank of the cove, not ten yards from the boat.

Lauren gasps. "Are those real?"

"You didn't grow up in Florida, did you, Lou?" I laugh. "But that video is twenty years old. Not many gators on Lake Lovelace these days."

Up on the screen, Amber asks, "How old were you when you first competed as a pro?"

"I was seventeen. It was a different sport back in the nineties, you know?"

Amber's questions stay focused on wakeboarding, then my work as a personal trainer, including footage of me and Jeremy at a bodybuilding competition he'd won.

"She brings out the best in me. Makes me work for it, takes my health and my limits seriously. She was born to do this."

The footage switches to the roller derby scrimmage back in August, and Amber's voice-over continues. "But Durham found a second wind for her own competitive spirit in the form of roller derby."

Me at practice, weaving through the cones of an obstacle course, then the image cuts back to the interview.

"What initially attracted you to the game?"

"Joe Mama, the coach. She made it sound badass and crazy fun. She talked about how it felt to be a part of a team—which is something I never really had before. And honestly, I missed competitive sports."

The questions turn to my retirement and transition, and I tune them out, instead peeking around at the rapt faces of my teammates. When I talk about feeling wrong in my skin, Bex's face twists up like she's going to cry.

When I point out that my wakeboard tournament winnings financed my medical transition, that I had to choose between transitioning and college, and that I was *lucky* and *privileged* to be able to make that choice, Stella nods and looks over at me. "I know that's right."

"Do you ever regret ending your wakeboarding career when and how you did? With a voluntary retirement?"

I glance up at the screen then, at myself. On-screen me shakes her head.

"When Ben Warren broke his back, it changed everything. For one, without my idol and best friend in the boat with me, it wasn't as much fun. For another, with him out of the way—" On-screen me laughs and gazes right into the camera. "Sorry, Ben! With Ben out of the competitions, I was winning more and able to save more money—enough to transition. When I retired, some would say I was at my peak. But for me the best thing about the sport was the time spent on the water with my friends, and that peaked when Ben and I were friendly rivals."

"And derby? What's the best thing about derby?"

"I think, for me, it's being accepted and included in female friendship, in a space that isn't dominated by men. In a space where our bodies aren't for decoration, and every body type has an advantage." On-screen me takes a drink of water and smiles at the camera.

"What's wonderful about derby is what makes it so beautifully subversive: it empowers women to love what our bodies can do."

"Hell yeah!" Lauren shouts, pumping her fist in the air. She jumps down from the high-top bar table where she's been sitting and rushes me for a hug as the credits roll.

Before I know it, the rest of the team is piling into my booth and onto the table to hug and kiss me.

Across from me, Joe laughs and holds the beers out of the way.

It's over, and my team loves me. I was afraid I might cry, but as I hug my friends—that's who they've become—I'm flying high from their affection and their company.

Riding back to Joe's place later—in her van because *I* have a buzz—with Elvis in my lap and the window rolled down, I let out a giggle of pure relief.

She glances over at me. "You were amazing. That was—that was crazy brave."

"No, it wasn't brave." I shake my head. "But it might have been crazy. I was scared to death. Still am."

"I'm sorry that you couldn't be open about our relationship. I want to tell the team, but I'm not sure when would be the right time. You understand, don't you?"

"I guess. I mean, eventually we *need* to tell them. It's not fair to expect Lauren to keep our secret, and I *have* been shacking up at your place for the last month."

"I know. I know. But with my history with Chloe . . ."

And that pisses me off. I've been fine with the secrecy—to a point. But now she's just making excuses.

"Your history with Chloe has fuck-all to do with you and me. And you quitting your former team to try to save your relationship with her has even less to do with me."

"I know! But Stella isn't going to see it that way."

"And Stella is fucking Bex, so who gives a fuck what she thinks?"

"I do. *I* give a fuck what my best friend thinks. I give a fuck about her trust. I can't— If Ben thought you were doing something shitty, wouldn't you give a fuck?"

My annoyance turns to ice-cold fury.

"So what, now our relationship is something shitty?"

"Don't put words in my mouth; that is not at *all* what I meant."

"It's what you fucking said."

"Okay, yeah, it's what I fucking said, but you know me well enough to know that's not what I fucking meant."

Our voices are rising, and hers is growing hoarser by the moment. And I hate it, because I want to yell and scream it out and get past the fighting to the kissing and making up—but I'm worried about her vocal cords.

"You know what? Don't strain yourself. I think we both need to cool off. Take me home, okay?"

"We're almost to my house. We'll go inside and talk it out."

"Don't you think we've hurt each other enough for one evening? Please take me home now."

She pulls the van into her driveway, cuts the engine, and looks at me. "Tina. Please?"

And that "please," especially when her voice cracks like *that*? It would usually be enough. But not tonight. I can't. I can't have this conversation now, because when it comes right down to it, I want her to choose me. I want her to choose derby *and* me. And if she can't even tell the team she and I are dating, on the night I told the whole world I used to have a dick? Then I don't know if it's ever going to happen. And I don't want to be the one who forces her to say that.

I pull my phone out of my purse and call my knight in shining armor.

"Ben, can you come get me?"

I manage to hold it together when she screws up her face and says, "Fine, fucking fine. I was proud of you tonight. I'm still proud of you. You want to put your feelings of shame and inadequacy on me, that's your deal."

I manage to hold it together when first the door to her van, and then the front door to her house slam shut.

But when Ben pulls up in Dave's Range Rover, and I put Elvis in the backseat, I lose it. With shaking hands, I open the passenger door and climb inside, and then the sobs come, racking my whole body with silent agony.

"Are you safe?" Ben reaches across the console and picks up my hand.

"Yes."

"Do you want to stay with me and Dave?"

On the one hand, there's the little house I shared with Lisa, and all the ways it still feels like ours and not mine, like there's a ghost living there with me. On the other, there's Ben's big house, and how he and Dave will be walking around giving each other besotted glances.

Rock. Hard place.

"Maybe I can sleep in your car," I mumble.

"I have every movie Linklater's ever made on DVD."

"Yeah?" I sit up straighter, remembering a time in the late nineties when Ben and I stayed up all night in some lame hotel in Orlando, watching *Before Sunrise* and talking about nothing and everything. "Do you have any Phish Food?"

"We can stop at Publix and get some."

And for a minute, it seems like drowning my tears in a pint of ice cream while watching movies is exactly what I need. But once again, it's Ben to the rescue, someone else fixing everything so I don't have to deal. It's time for me to start taking responsibility.

I shake my head. "I'm gonna be okay. I don't need babysitting."

"Honey, Dave and I watched your interview—which was amazing, by the way. You might not need babysitting, but I bet you'd like company. It's okay to need people."

"I *need* to be alone."

"If that's what you want."

"It really is."

A few minutes after I walk in the door, my phone rings. Joe.

I think about letting it go to voice mail, but at the last minute I pick up.

Her voice is rough like she's been crying. "I'm sorry, Tina. You were right."

"I don't want to be right, but I don't want to keep our relationship a secret anymore, either. We're going to keep fighting about it and hurting each other, and that sucks, Joe. It's not who you are and it's not who I am."

"I need more time. I need—"

"How much would be enough? Two weeks? A month? Until the beginning of the season? Or, better yet, the end of the season next June?"

"I don't know how much!" Her voice cracks on the word "know." The line is quiet for a moment.

Finally, I say, "Secrets always come out. They're like—like a heart condition you're born with but don't know about, until the stress is too much and you have a cardiac event."

"I can't— I'm not ready."

"I know. And I get that, Joe, but I don't think we can keep doing this. Maybe we should just walk away now."

I want to take the words back. They hang there on the line, and they choke me from my own throat. Every fiber of my being is screaming that I'm a fuckup, that I'm wrong, that I'm destroying a chance to be happy.

"Walk away—you mean break up?"

Her voice cracks again—is she crying? I don't want to break up. I don't want to make her cry.

And now it's too late.

"I'm sorry, Joe."

"Why are you sorry? I keep hurting you without meaning to. Why are you sorry?" Her sharp gasps tell me I was right, she *is* crying, and I hate it, but like before, it's that catch in her voice that firms up my resolve. I need her to choose me, and I can't make her do it.

"I'm sorry it can't be different."

"Will you still play derby?"

I sit down in the doorway to my kitchen and let my head drop against the wall. "Of course I will."

"It's going to be really hard."

I know she's not talking about the sport.

"Treat me like one of the other girls. Treat me like Stella or Bex. Don't do that cold-shoulder thing you tried before."

"I won't. God, Tina, I'm so sorry."

"Me too."

"So, I'll see you at practice?"

"Yeah."

She apologizes again through the good-byes, and I set the phone on the floor. Elvis, leash still clipped to his collar, stares at me from across the room. I lift my hand, and he stands up and comes over to me, nudging my hand with his head and whining.

I wrap my arms around his warm little body and sob into his fur.

# chapter THIRTEEN

"**r**esuming regular workouts" in two weeks was optimistic of Jeremy's doctors. Pouring sweat, he steps off the treadmill after a short run and glares at me. It's a month past his ablation and he looks ready to throw something.

"Am I free to go now?"

"How are you feeling?"

"I just ran my slowest mile in three years, and I feel like I ran a marathon. My whole body hurts. I'm so tired I could literally lie down and fall asleep on the floor. In other words? Like shit."

"So, recovery is going well."

He starts stretching, wincing when he gets to his left leg. "Seriously? At the rate it's going, I'm never going to compete again."

"Feeling sorry for yourself. How's that working out for you?"

"You can be a real bitch, you know that?"

"And deflecting. Nice. Come on, Jeremy, what're you really mad about?"

"My body fucking sucks right now!" he shouts, then he laughs and buries his hands in his hair. He looks at me, still laughing. "God, it felt good to say that."

"It's temporary. Your heart, man. You had a procedure done on your *heart*."

"But it's fixed. It was weak before, now it's strong, and I'm the complete fucking opposite. It's not fair."

"You want to shout some more?"

He shakes his head. "Honestly, I just want a nap."

"Okay. I'll see you at our regular time on Thursday. Don't be too hard on yourself."

He goes off to the showers and I head up to the front of the gym to make notes on his progress on the computer. I'm just finishing up when the door swings open and a pair of familiar faces walk in.

"Chase, Lauren, this is a surprise." I hit Save and come around the desk to greet them.

"It took me a while—" Lauren holds up the business card I gave her at the scrimmage in Orlando. "But I wanted to sign up for personal training—maybe we can focus on ways that I can skate faster?"

Oh, thank God. Nate's going to be thrilled. "That's—that's fantastic. Absolutely."

"Me too." Chase smiles at his wife. "Because if I'm going to learn how to ref, I should learn how to keep up with you all. It's something Lou and I can do together."

I should buy a lottery ticket. I don't think my luck could get any better.

"Okay, well, we can start the paperwork to get you into the system. Personal training clients have regular use of the gym too; it's included in my fee. And then we'll talk about your fitness goals."

As I'm getting the new member paperwork for them, Jeremy comes out of the locker room, still pale and drawn, but smiling sheepishly.

"Thank you." He pulls me into a hug. "Em and my mom have been fussing and fawning over me, and I think I needed someone to let me get mad."

And God, I can relate to that. A wave of anger hits me all over again, like the moment I first realized that the world was arbitrary and our bodies weren't part of some grand design, but what we ended up with through luck and genetics.

"You're gonna be okay. This machine of yours—" I punch his shoulder lightly "—might have come from the factory not the way you wanted. But you've fine-tuned the shit out of it, and it's going to run strong for a lot of years."

He nods. "You're good at this, you know?"

Embarrassed, I shrug off the compliment. "I like what I do. I like helping people get strong."

"Looks like you got two new ones to work with." He gestures with his chin toward where Lauren and Chase wait.

The grin feels like it's going to split my face. "My derby teammate and her husband. They want me to train them."

"Good. I'll see you Thursday."

I wave good-bye to him and bring the paperwork to Lauren and Chase. For a while, there's only the *scritch scratch* of pen on paper.

"Where are your kids?" I ask. "Don't you homeschool?"

"They go to a math and science co-op on Tuesdays and Thursdays." Lauren glances up from the paperwork. "We're kind of hoping that we can schedule our training sessions on those days."

I glance around the empty gym. "I think we can manage."

"Can I talk to you about Joe?"

My stomach sinks and flops.

Chase meets my gaze and holds up his hands. "I am Switzerland."

"Okay, what about her?"

Lauren picks at the sleeve of her shirt for a minute, then peeks up at me. "Well, I saw you guys that night . . . and lately she's been down, you know?"

I flinch. Practices have been strained for both of us. She'll say something funny, and I'll laugh and reach for a hug, and then she'll go quiet and skate away. She and Stella have spent a lot of time huddled up in corners, talking, and I doubt it's all strategy related. "Yeah, I noticed."

"And I wanted to say if you guys broke up or something because of what I saw, I'm sorry. I didn't mean to barge in on you and I've felt awful ever since."

"We didn't break up because of you. Please don't feel bad about it."

"But you did break up? That's why she's sad, isn't it?"

Her words are like a knife in my gut and she won't stop twisting it. "Lauren, it's really complicated. I started falling for her for all the wrong reasons."

"Like what?"

"Seriously?"

She shrugs. "A little post-bout analysis. Except with relationships. Think of me as your relationship coach."

"I like how she fixes things. Not just for her job—but that's perfect for her, actually. She's always looking for ways to make things better. But see, what I *need* is to be able to fix my own shit."

"You're crazy. That sounds like a *good* reason to fall for someone."

Chase leans over and stage whispers, "Says the wife of a handyman."

Swatting his arm, she turns back to me. "No, I see what you mean. What else?"

"When I'm with her—she doesn't make me feel big and clumsy. She makes me feel sexy and cherished and *wanted*."

"Again, I'm not seeing the downside. Those are pretty awesome feelings."

"And even though it's why we broke up, there's that thrill of being with someone secretly. It's kind of hot—but that's not enough. Not if she won't ever come out and say she wants to be with me to the people who matter most."

"Here." Lauren reaches into her purse and pulls out a tissue. I wipe my eyes and shake my head.

"I'm sorry."

"Don't be, I asked."

I change the subject then, asking about the kids, and they both start talking excitedly about bringing them to the exhibition bout the following week—my first bout, and I'm skating pivot. Also, my first chance to skate directly against Joe's ex.

By the time they leave, with their first appointment made for Thursday, right after Jeremy's, I feel a little less like going home and spending the rest of the day crying into Elvis's fur.

# chapter FOURTEEN

It's supposed to be my first bout as pivot, but the night before, Stella drops a keg on her foot and fractures the second metatarsal. Who fractures the second metatarsal?

As we're warming up on the track the morning of the bout, Joe pulls me and Bex aside and says, "Hey, I know it feels like the deck is stacked against us. Paula Fast One is . . . fuck. She's fucking fast. I think our best bet against her is to have the most experienced blockers out there. Which means, Bex . . ."

"I skate pivot. Hooch, we practiced you getting the panty on your head. We didn't practice passing it the other way."

Me. Jammer. *Holy shit.* It's a lot of responsibility, and I turn to Joe to tell her she's crazy and I'm not ready, but the way she looks at me, like she's got no doubts—it goes a long way toward calming mine.

"It's okay." I shake my head and smile at Bex. "If I need to get it in your hand, I'll do my best. But I think my strategy is going to be to skate like hell, right?"

"Remember to stay low." Joe meets my gaze, all intense. "You're taller than anyone else on that track except maybe Paula. Get low, stay low. Swing to the outside of the pack as much as possible to pass. Don't break to the inside unless there's a clear opening. And for fuck's sake, don't forget how to jump."

Like I have any choice?

The first jam is a blur. Paula leads it while I'm still getting my tits and ass grabbed on the line. I finally break free of the blockers, but she's already scoring points; seconds later, she puts her hands on her hips to call off the jam right as I'm about to lap my first opponent. Shut out in my first jam.

"It's okay, T. Not your fault." Lauren murmurs as we line up again.

This time, Lauren hits Paula with an unholy fury, skating in front of her and bouncing up to plant her shoulder in Paula's chest. Paula goes down in my peripheral vision and I see my opening. I feint left, lurch right, and skate like hell for the gap narrowing between two blockers in yellow.

By some outrageous fucking miracle, I'm leading the jam.

Blood pounds in my ears as I close in on the pack. The cheers of the crowd are deafening. Somewhere out there, my best friends in the world are watching this. Knowing Ben and Eddie are seeing me race toward the pack makes me brave.

"Butt down, Hooch!" someone shouts.

I spot Bex ahead of me, and for a split second, I think about handing her the panty and letting her take over the jam. Instead, I reach for her hips, grab them, and use her momentum to slingshot myself forward.

How many have I passed?

Fuck if I know. I push toward the inside of the turn and then—*bam*!—hit the floor.

The ref calls a penalty on the girl who blocked me, but my brain is scattered. Joe pulls me out.

Bex takes over as jammer.

Joe puts me back in once I've caught my breath, and this time she puts me in the pivot position. I toe up to the line and feel Lauren behind me. She leans forward so our asses are practically rubbing together.

"Don't get any ideas, straight girl," I tease, loudly enough for the other team's skaters to hear it. Lauren laughs, the whistle blows, and Bex puts her shoulder into one of the other team's blockers to break free.

Lauren and I are hip to hip now, a last line of defense against Paula Fast One.

She leans left; I feint right. Paula goes for the space opening between us and I cut back to the left and swing in front of her.

She lurches onto Lauren's shoulder while Bex starts collecting points.

Halftime is a blur of earnest advice and shoulder thumping and chugging Gatorade. Is this actually happening? By some miracle, we're winning.

The miracle holds.

At the final buzzer, the other girls swarm me with hugs and pats on my helmet. I'm swept up in a tide of enthusiasm unlike anything I've ever felt before. I look around for Joe, and finally meet her eyes over the crowd.

Something in her smile feels like a hello, and a blessing, and a hug all at once.

Spent and sweaty after the bout, I skate out to where we'll meet the fans.

Signing autographs isn't new for me, and that makes it weird when Lauren tries to give me pointers.

"Remember, they're here for the persona. You're not Tina Durham, you're Hoochie Glide."

"Lou. I've been signing autographs since I was seventeen," I whisper. "And I had a persona then, too."

She turns beet red, blushing all the way to the roots of her hair. "I was only trying to help."

Oh shit. Now I feel like an asshole. "I didn't mean— I'm sorry. Come on, Lauren, don't be mad, okay? I hate it when you're mad."

"I'm not mad, I'm embarrassed."

"Well, don't be embarrassed. You're awesome, you're like—" And I remember then, something Stella said about Joe weeks before, the best friend she had out there. "You're my derby wife."

She looks up at me, wide-eyed, and her mouth drops open. "Yeah?"

"Yeah."

She hugs me, and I think she might be crying, and I'm *definitely* getting misty, but I hug her back.

Then the doors swing open and the kids start charging us. *Fans.* And holy shit, are they different from wakeboarding fans. For one thing, there are a lot of girls. Not just women and teenagers, but *girls.* And they want my autograph.

"Tina!"

I look up from signing a helmet, and I'm greeted by a really welcome sight. Ben, Wish, and Eddie approach, all smiles. I say good-bye to the little girl, handing her back her Sharpie, and turn to hug my friends.

Eddie squeezes me extra tight, then wrinkles up his nose and says "Ew, girl sweat."

"I'm so glad you guys made it!"

Ben rubs one side of his face and gives me an apologetic smile. "Dave's sorry he couldn't come. He's in Charleston dealing with the wedding stuff. You remember how that goes."

Mostly, I remember being absolutely fucking terrified. But who wants to tell a groom-to-be that?

"I do, though, honestly, Lisa took care of most of it." *Like she took care of everything.* A few months ago, that thought would have brought with it a wave of guilt and remorse. But today, it feels matter-of-fact—like I'm seeing my former relationship for what it was, *without* the guilt. I smile at Ben. "Damn, I can't believe the wedding is two weeks away."

A big, goofy grin crosses his face. "Me neither."

I turn to Eddie. "So, what did you think, Mr. Anti-Jock? Did you have a good time?"

"I loved watching you have so much fun, but there are more pleasant ways to collect bruises. *Ahem.*"

Behind him, I catch sight of Joe, deep in conversation with Chloe, who has one hand on Joe's shoulder as she laughs. Seeing them together so intimately, even in a crowd, breaks something inside me. All the blood in my body seems to rush in my ears, and even though Eddie's boyfriend is talking now, I don't hear a word.

"Good-bye, Eddie!" Eddie says, clearly in response to Wish's prompting, and then they're leaving.

"See you at the wedding, T!" Eddie shouts over his shoulder, and then it's just me and Ben.

"So. Which one is she?" Ben peers around. "Your girl?"

"She's not my girl." *Not anymore.* "But that's her." I gesture with my chin. He glances over his shoulder, does a double take at the sight of Joe and Chloe.

"She has a nice smile," he says tactfully. "Do we hate her?"

I laugh and shake my head. "It would be easier if we did. But I like her too much."

A kid—maybe seven or eight years old—wearing jeans, a white T, and gender-neutral ponytail, approaches with Mom hovering like a wary, watchful dragon. They hold up a tiny pair of skates.

"Sign my boots?"

I kneel down to be at their height.

"Sure, sweetheart. What's your name?"

They turn to their mom, who smiles and whispers something in their ear.

"I'm Thomas to friends." They puff out their chest. "And family. Mom says you're family."

I look up at her sharply, and she nods. "I'm Sarah. And I'm trying to be a good ally for my child."

"Thomas, do you like to be called he?" I start doodling a roller-skating person on the skate.

"I don't like to be called he or she. My teachers call me she."

*Dear Thomas,*

*Always be proud to be yourself.*

*Your friend,*

*Tina "Hoochie Glide" Durham*

"I had another name once. But that's not who I am." I keep doodling—stars like the jammer's helmet.

"You're *Hoochie Glide!*" Thomas shouts it, and everyone laughs, but I want them to know—I want them to understand that I get them.

"I'm also Tina Durham, and I'm so happy to meet you, Thomas." I give their little hand a serious handshake, with some complicated snaps and twists and slaps.

"Thank you," Sarah whispers fervently. "You're the first trans person they've met. We saw your special on *Weekend Sports*, and Tommy . . . oh God, they were so happy. They shrieked and shouted about how you were—please forgive them if this is offensive, I don't think they understood *everything*—a boy when you wakeboarded, and a lady when you skate. I explained that it was different for you, that you were always a lady, but it was secret for a while. But they saw . . ."

"They saw trans, and they saw themself." I take her hand. Seeing someone emotional like this for their kid always gets me right in the gut. "It's okay, I completely and totally understand. Can I—can I hug you?"

She grabs me then, and holds on like her life depends on it. "Thank you so much for what you've done today."

"I skated a tough bout. I shook your kid's hand, and I believed in them, that's all. I'm so happy I met Thomas today."

"May I take a picture?" Joe comes up behind me but addresses Sarah. "I'm happy to send a copy to you for Thomas—but I think Hoochie would like one too."

"We would love that, thank you." Sarah leans over and says something to Thomas, who nods.

We huddle together for the camera, their little arm around my shoulders. Before the shutter clicks, they tell me they want to use boy words someday, but they aren't ready yet.

"I didn't use girl words until I was all grown up," I whisper. "You can use 'they' as long as you want. It's yours. Don't let anyone take it from you."

"I won't."

We pinky swear over it while Joe gets Sarah's email address.

"I'll email you the picture too," Joe says, showing it to me on the back of the camera.

"I'd like that, thank you. Oh, and you have to meet Ben!"

He moved out of the way while I was talking to Thomas, but now he steps forward and gives Joe his most charming smile.

"Ben Warren. Nice to meet you."

"Joe Delario." She shakes his hand and sort of sizes him up. "So you're *the* Ben Warren. Local legend."

He blushes and turns to me. "She's met Eddie already?"

"No, baby, she lives in Lake Lovelace. The whole town is proud of you."

"Aw, hell."

"I think you embarrassed him." Joe laughs. "I'm happy to meet you too, Ben. I've heard so much about you, and all of it was good."

"In that case, Tina left out the really scandalous stories."

"Excuse me for interrupting." Chloe comes up to us. "Joe, I'm leaving now. Call me next week, okay?"

"You got it. Thanks hon." Joe gives her a big hug. They look good together, and I hate it. I hate that she's hugging her ex right in front of me like it's no big deal. I hate that they make a cute couple. I hate that they're apparently going to talk on the phone, and I hate that I ended it with Joe before it could hurt, because this hurts too, and it hurts so much worse because it's my fault.

"Bye, Hoochie. Great skating today." Chloe waves and walks away.

Joe turns to Ben. "Are you going to join us at the party tonight at Blue's?"

Ben looks startled for a minute, then shakes his head. "I'm sorry, I'm not comfortable in party environments. I don't drink."

"Oh, well, we'll miss you. I was hoping to hear some of *Tina's* scandalous stories."

"Oh God, Ben, get out of here." I shove him toward the door. He gives me one last hug, and then he goes, smiling on his way out.

"So, um, do you want to ride with me?" Her voice is small and shy behind the rasp. "I've really missed you."

She's carefully not meeting my gaze. I take in her hunched body language, not her usual swagger, and it feels so wrong that she's humbling herself just to ask for my company.

"Joe . . ."

"Please?"

And how can I say no?

"I have to go home and shower. Pick me up at seven?"

She smiles and her shoulders drop with relief. "Yeah?"

"You know I'm a sucker for the way your voice cracks when you say please."

"Ooh, maybe I should practice and see if I can make it crack every time." She laughs and squeezes my hand. "I'll see you at seven."

# chapter FIFTEEN

I have a doorbell, but she knocks. Soft, like she's calling my name.

When I open the door, she's leaning on my entryway in skinny jeans, a button-down, and suspenders, with her hair slicked back and a grin on her face.

The swagger has returned.

"You look—" I shake my head, searching for the words. "You look amazing. Dapper as fuck. Come on in, I need to—"

She puts her hand on my arm and I stop babbling. Even this little touch, this tiny contact, is enough to set my heart racing.

"Are you nervous?" she asks.

I nod.

She follows me into the house and shuts the door behind her. "You look really nice."

I glance down at my shirtdress. The same one she—

"I fixed the button," I blurt out.

"I'm glad it was repairable. I'm sorry I wasn't more careful."

"It's okay. It was hot." I laugh. "Let me grab Elvis and my purse."

During the drive to the bar, she hums "Suspicious Minds." When she realizes I'm listening, she blushes and stops. "Your dog gives me the worst earworms."

We enter the bar to a chorus of "Hooch!" and "Joe!"

It hits me all at once: she's delivered on everything she promised when we first met for drinks after she fixed my washing machine. Friendship, teamwork, female companionship. Something bigger than individual glory. A lump forms in my throat, and I cover it by going to the bar and asking Stella for some water for Elvis.

She gives me a once-over as I stand there waiting, then glances at Joe. "You and Joe came together?"

"Yeah, you know—a designated driver thing." The lie tastes awkward in my mouth—but is it a lie? It feels like one.

"Uh-huh." She watches Joe across the room as she says the next part. "You skated well today. I'm proud of you."

"Thanks."

"But you're only keeping my spot warm. I'm coming back."

I laugh. "I am happy to be pivot to your jammer."

She gives a sharp little nod and then looks down at Elvis.

"We need to get him a purple LLRG doggie T-shirt. He's awfully underdressed to be our mascot." She hands me the water and a basket of fried pickles. "Would you give these to Joe for me? I'll be out there to join y'all in a minute. Stupid crutches."

Lauren and Bex are deep in conversation over by the jukebox, and by the time I get to Joe, they've picked a song, the bar is filling with music, and tables are being shoved aside to make a dance floor.

"Dance with me?" Joe asks as I set the pickles on the table. "It would seem weird if we didn't."

"I'd dance with you anyway." I let Elvis off leash, and he hops up onto the seat of our usual booth and settles in.

There's something gentle and sweet in the way Joe holds me while we dance, like she can't believe I'm there. She keeps smiling up at me and biting her lip.

"What's going on?" I ask, unable to stop smiling back at her.

"I'm just really happy. We won our bout. You're dancing with me."

I pull her a little closer, and she puts her arms around my neck. Our breasts are pushed together, and my breath catches in my throat. "I meant what I said earlier. You look pretty tonight."

"Thanks." Then she closes her eyes, and we sway together, and I want to kiss her so badly, I don't know if I can take it. Thankfully, the song ends, and Bex cuts in. It seems like I dance with everyone except Stella, since she's on crutches. When I dance with Chase, it's the first time I'm not the taller partner.

"This is nice, dancing with a dude." I smile up at him. "I should try it more often."

"It's kind of weird dancing with the girl who makes me do my pushups," he grumbles, then raises an eyebrow at me. "Unless you think I could skip them."

"Don't let him, Tina!" Lauren calls. "I like his guns!"

He laughs as he spins me under his arm. "I guess I have you to thank for giving Joe the idea of having me ref."

"I didn't do—"

"Don't lie to me, girl." His voice is stern, but he's grinning as he says it. "You don't even see—you sat here in this room, while all these people who love you watched you go on television and tell the world who you are and why you matter. And you don't even see it."

"See what?" I look around. "I'm just me."

"Well, if you can't see it, I don't know if I can help you." He smiles.

"I'm going to give you extra pushups for that."

"You worry that you need people too much, but the way I see it, other people need you—to motivate them, to show them where to find their courage. Yes, they still have to put in the work, but they *want* to because *you* believe they can."

"That's what a personal trainer does."

"Yeah, but you don't save all your mojo for work. You do it *all* the time. Lauren says she only made the team that night because you talked her down."

"She'd have made it anyway."

"Eventually, sure. But she thinks it happened when it did because of you."

Then the song ends, and I beg off the next dance, heading for the ladies' room to catch my breath and figure out what he meant by that pretty speech.

It's empty, and I take a moment to splash some cold water on my face, which is flushed from dancing and laughing and beer. *I help people?*

"Hey."

With the water running, I hadn't heard the door open, but there's Joe, leaning on the wall by the paper towel dispenser.

"Hi."

She waves her hand in front of the dispenser's motion sensor, rips off the towel, and hands it to me. Dabbing the water off my face, I stare at her.

"Please—"

"I miss—"

We both start laughing, then the next thing I know, she's in my arms, and I'm pressed back against the wall, and we're kissing, really kissing, like we'll die if we don't.

"I missed you," I gasp when she bites my neck.

She groans and tilts her head back when I run my hands over her nipples. "God, yes." She practically climbs my body, shoving her knee between my legs.

My skirt rides up and I haul her closer, our bodies rocking together in frantic rhythm. I slip her suspenders off one shoulder and start tugging her shirt out of her pants.

Then the door bursts open and we break apart, panting.

Some people never learn their lessons.

"What the fuck are you doing?" Stella crosses her arms over her chest.

"Stella..." I start, then I look at Joe, who's gorgeous and disheveled with the suspender slipped off. I smile at her, and she giggles, running a hand through her slicked-back hair.

"I'm kissing my girlfriend; give us some privacy," she says, still laughing.

"Your girlfriend?" I feel a thrill even though, no, we haven't talked about that. She just called me her girlfriend. To Stella. To her derby wife.

To her best friend who's injured and can't skate, and resents her old girlfriend.

"Joe—" I start again, but Stella interrupts me.

"I can't fucking believe you're doing this again. Don't shit where you eat, Joe. Don't fuck your teammates. Because once you get past the heart-eyes and rainbows phase, you're going to walk the fuck out. Not on her, never on *her*. You'll walk out on everybody else."

I close my eyes and my head falls back against the wall with a *thunk*. "That's pretty rich coming from you. Aren't you and Bex a thing?"

"I didn't walk out on you." Joe pinches the skin at the bridge of her nose. "Derby wasn't fun anymore."

"We were the top seed in the league." Stella's voice goes loud and pleading.

"So what?" Joe throws out her arms. "So what? My girlfriend and I were fighting, you were pissed that she's a better jammer than you, and you blamed me for *everything*. It didn't matter that we were the top seed. I needed a goddamn break. Why do you think that when I came back, when I started *this* team, I didn't fucking skate?"

Stella reels back. "We lost the semifinals because you quit. And now what? You're making the same mistake all over again with a brand-new team. You keep giving me derby teams to love and then abandoning us."

*Ouch.*

"Oh my fucking God, Stella. I am not some god of derby. I just want to have a good time. Yeah, I wanna fucking win, who doesn't? But you didn't lose because *I* wasn't skating. You lost because the other team skated better that day. Exactly how we won today because our girls skated their asses off."

Stella starts to say something, but I can't watch them shred their friendship like this anymore.

"Stop." I hold up both hands. "Stella. When Joe started a new team, did she ask Chloe to be a part of it?"

Joe scoffs behind me.

"No." Stella mutters and looks away.

"Joe, is Stella your best friend in the whole world?"

"Yeah. She fucking is."

"Okay, so stop bitching at each other about what's done. Tell each other what's really important."

They stare at me for a minute. Then at each other.

"Don't worry; I'll go wait outside."

I straighten my dress, make sure all the buttons are secure, and head back to the party.

Back in the bar, I collect Elvis and take him outside, Chase's words from earlier running through my mind. *"They still have to put in the work, but they* want *to because you* believe they can." Like Lauren and her 27/5. Like getting Jeremy back on track after his ablation.

Like believing Joe and Stella can fix their friendship.

Have I been trying too hard to fix everything myself—pushing people away when they just wanted to be there for me? Maybe, all this time, I've been worried not about the way Lisa fixed things for me, but that if she couldn't fix it, our marriage wasn't fixable. And did that mean *I* was broken?

But I'm *not* broken. I'm the girl who believes in people. And sometimes they believe in me back.

"Hey."

I give Elvis a little more slack on his leash and turn around—there she is. My Joe.

Her suspender is still down, but she's tucked in her shirt. She's beautiful.

"Everything okay?"

"Almost."

"What did you tell her about you and me?"

"I told her the truth, that I have a heart condition. It's one of those sneaky ones you don't realize you have until it wrecks you."

I look down at Elvis and try to fight the smile. Hell. I can't play it cool. Heart on my sleeve, whatever condition it's in.

"Is it serious?"

"I think . . ." Her voice breaks a little; she licks her lips and glances away, then back at me, all intense and gorgeous. "I think the actual diagnosis is 'twitterpated,' but I might need a second opinion, because I'm also showing symptoms of 'smitten.'"

"Wow, you should definitely get that checked out. It sounds serious."

"Very, very serious."

"What treatment do they prescribe for this?"

"Well, that's the thing. I hear kiss therapy is showing some promise."

Her kiss is soft, and sweet, and I can feel her smiling against my lips.

I pull back and touch her smile with one finger, trace it, catch myself smiling back.

"What's going to happen now, with you and me?"

"Well, your derby wife knows. And my derby wife knows. And I told everyone else before I came out here that I wanted to date you, and if any of them had a problem with it, I would make them do suicide sprints on Monday night—"

"You did *not*!"

She laughs in my arms. "No. But I did tell them my personal life, and yours, aren't up for debate."

"And Stella? What about her?"

"Stella is hurt. It's not about you—except in the sense that you're the reason this is coming up now. A catalyst, or whatever. We have work to do, you know?"

I nod. "Do you want me to talk to her?"

She shakes her head. "No, not tonight. I want to take you home and work on that kissing therapy thing more."

My heart seems to flutter in my chest. "I told you, that first night we came here, that I didn't think I should get involved in a complicated thing. I was wrong. Between you and skating and everything, this summer was the best—complicated, yeah, but the *best* summer. Even the weeks when we weren't together were amazing. I feel like I'm a part of something now."

Her smile lights up her face. "You are. It wasn't just a summer thing for me. I mean, it's October now, and we're going into the skating season. If it was just a summer thing for you, and you want to focus on the skating, I understand, but—"

I cut her off with a kiss, then say, "It wasn't just a summer thing for me either."

"Then let's go home."

# epilogue

When the whistle blows, I'm sprawled out in a tangle of limbs, one of Paula Fast One's locs tickling my ear.

"Damn, Hooch, you can really hit," she wheezes around her mouth guard as we struggle to untangle ourselves. "Was that your penalty, or mine?"

We clashed so hard, neither of us managed to fall small, and if this were a real match, we'd have both been sent to the penalty box for endangering the other players. As it is, we're supposed to be demonstrating—as vividly as possible—the importance of safe falls.

Joe skates over to us and reaches out a hand. I grab it first— girlfriend's prerogative—and then turn to help Chloe to her feet.

"Okay, so, *that* is an example of how *not* to fall, courtesy of Hoochie Glide and Paula Fast One." Stella's voice is full of mirth as she explains to the Central Florida Derby Campers what just happened. "Y'all know what's coming next though, right?"

The campers groan.

"Not suicides!" Thomas pipes up, throwing me a desperate glare.

"You shouldn't have said anything," the girl next to them says. "Now we're going to have to."

"Yes, suicides. But first, let's give a great big Derby Camp thanks to Hoochie Glide and Paula Fast One!" Stella claps her wrist guards together and the campers follow her lead, the plastic echoes of their clapping filling the roller-skating rink.

I give the kids a wave, and so does Chloe, and then we skate away, following Joe off the floor.

"Are you both okay?" Joe waits for us to catch up and then wraps her arm around my waist when we reach her.

"Fine." I grin at her.

"I'm going for an ice pack." Chloe shakes her head. "My ass *hurts*."

We say our good-byes, and Joe and I skate over to the water fountain off to the side of the rink. After taking a few deep gulps of water, I wipe my mouth and grin again.

"That was fun."

She laughs. "Your boss is on cloud nine. He stopped by to watch the demonstrations."

"Nate did?" Oh *God*. Derby Camp had been my idea. I brought it up as a possible revenue stream—and he'd given me free rein to run with it. "He was really nervous about the liability stuff. Just yesterday he pulled me aside during a weight session to tell me he thought we were going to get sued."

"He's fine, I promise. Katie went over everything with him before we opened the doors this morning. He's never run a program for kids before; he'll get used to it." She grins wickedly. "He'll have to. We have a waiting list for the next three preteen sessions, and teenagers are sold out six months in advance."

*Holy shit.*

"So..."

"So your boss and Katie just found ways to keep both their respective businesses open thanks to your brilliant idea. And we're training up the next generation of Lake Lovelace Rollergirls."

"And boys and enbies," I add.

"And boys and enbies."

She leans in and kisses me, and even though we haven't hidden these kisses for months, I still get that thrill from kissing her—the same sweet rush of heat and longing. It was never the secrecy that made it special.

"I love you," I murmur against her lips.

"Yeah," she sighs, and then nips at my earlobe. "Love you too."

Somewhere behind us, plastic wrist guards clap together, children shriek, and wheels hum along the wooden floor.

I've got my arms full of Joe—and it hits me all over again. This is my life, and it's real and it's fine.

Explore the rest of the *Lake Lovelace* series:
riptidepublishing.com/titles/univcrsc/lake-lovelace

Dear Reader,

Thank you for reading Vanessa North's *Roller Girl*!

We know your time is precious and you have many, many entertainment options, so it means a lot that you've chosen to spend your time reading. We really hope you enjoyed it.

We'd be honored if you'd consider posting a review—good or bad—on sites like **Amazon, Barnes & Noble, Kobo, Goodreads, Twitter, Facebook, Tumblr,** and your blog or website. We'd also be honored if you told your friends and family about this book. Word of mouth is a book's lifeblood!

For more information on upcoming releases, author interviews, blog tours, contests, giveaways, and more, please sign up for our weekly, spam-free newsletter and visit us around the web:

**Newsletter:** tinyurl.com/RiptideSignup
**Twitter:** twitter.com/RiptideBooks
**Facebook:** facebook.com/RiptidePublishing
**Goodreads:** tinyurl.com/RiptideOnGoodreads
**Tumblr:** riptidepublishing.tumblr.com

Thank you so much for Reading the Rainbow!

RiptidePublishing.com

# acknowledgments

Many thanks to May and Sam for beta reading, and to Courtney for assistance with all things derby. This book couldn't have happened without you all.

#TeamTina, your encouragement—especially yours, G—kept me going through several difficult rewrites and it means the world to me. Thank you!

And as always, huge thanks to my brilliant editor Caz—my books are so much stronger thanks to your guidance.

# ALSO BY vanessa north

Blueberry Boys
Hostile Beauty
The Dark Collector
High and Tight
The Lonely Drop

*Lake Lovelace Universe*
Double Up
Rough Road

How We Began: A Song for Sweater-boy
Lucky's Charms: Seamus
Love in the Cards: Two of Wands